MW01228723

DAMASCUS

A Full-Length Drama About . . . Signs of the Times

by Lowery Christopher Collins

DAMASCUS

A Full-Length Drama About . . . Signs of the Times

by Lowery Christopher Collins

Ponderlake
Publishing

DAMASCUS,
A FULL-LENGTH DRAMA ABOUT . . . SIGNS OF THE TIMES

Written by Lowery Christopher Collins

Ponderlake Publishing: www.ponderlake.com

Playwright and/or Royalty Information: www.ChristopherCollinsOnline.com

ISBN 978-0-9992241-9-9

DAMASCUS
by L. Christopher Collins

TOTAL, EXPANDED Cast of Characters (in order of appearance):

Jacob Bradford
Jeremiah Coffee
Caleb Martinez
  (first as bound man)
Soldier 1
Soldier 2
Kidnapper 1
Protester 1
Protester 2
Protester 3
Assassin
Assassinated Man
Citizen 1
Citizen 2
Isabel Coffee
Man 1
James Pennington
Lisa Pennington
Mandy Barlow
Intern
Eli Connor
Charlie
Partygoer 1
Betty Trevino
Dmitri Kovalenko
Partygoer 2
Announcer
Claudia Barker
Late Night Comedian
Nathan Pennington
YouTuber
Ruth
Actor 1

Church Worker 1
Church Worker 2
Speaker 1: an effeminate man
Speaker 2: a hunter
Speaker 3: emo girl
Speaker 4: older white man in suit
Speaker 5: Arab man
Speaker 6: youth in hoody
Speaker 7: college professor
Lydia Coffee
Circus Worker 2
Circus Worker 1
Circus Visitor 1
Circus Visitor 2
RC Montgomery
Young Jeremiah Coffee
Angela Goodson, reporter
Abel Montgomery
Andrea Lanier
Teacher
Doctor
Trey Grierson
Lt. Col. Alex Marshall
A marine
Man in Towel
Townsperson 1
Townsperson 2
Student Delivering Pledge
(Secret Service)
Agent 2 (Secret Service)

Senator Alan Michaels
Teenager 1
Teenager 2
Teenager 3
Frank, a teenager
Donna Martinez
David Martinez
Rosa Barrett
Syrian Man 1
Syrian Man 2
Harold Newford
Lt. Col. Mark Tamberol
Jones
Man 1
Newscaster
Final Reporter
Agent 1

THIS PLAY IS WRITTEN SO THAT ALL SEVENTY-SEVEN CHARACTERS CAN BE PLAYED BY ONLY _FIFTEEN_ ACTORS (NINE MALES AND SIX FEMALES.)

11

THE IDEAL BREAKDOWN OF CHARACTERS INTO FIFTEEN ACTORS IS AS FOLLOWS:

MALE #1: Jeremiah Coffee

MALE #2: Caleb Martinez/Bound Man in Scene 1

MALE #3: Jacob Bradford/Senator Alan Michaels/Jones

MALE #4: James Pennington/Man in Towel/Teenager 3/David Martinez/
Lt. Colonel Mark Tamberol/Speaker 4

MALE #5: Protester 1/Partygoer 2/Announcer/Church Worker 2/
The Child Jeremiah Coffee/Church Member 1/Harold Newford

MALE #6: Protester 2/Nathan/Circus Worker 1/Trey Grierson/Secret Service Agent 1

MALE #7: Soldier 1/Eli Connor/RC Montgomery/Marine 1/Student/
Teenager 2/Syrian Man 2/Speaker 2

MALE #8: Soldier 2/Dmitri Kovalenko/Circus Worker 2/
Abel Montgomery/Townsperson 1/Frank/Speaker 1

MALE #9: Kidnapper 1/Citizen 1/Charlie/Late-Night Comedian/Actor 1/
Lt. Colonel Alex Marshall/Teenager 1/Syrian Man 1/Man
1/Newscaster/Speaker 5/Secret Service Agent 2

FEMALE #1: Isabel Coffee/Assassinated Man/Intern

FEMALE #2: Betty Trevino/Reporter/Andrea Lanier/Speaker 7

FEMALE #3: Donna Martinez/(Syrian) Woman with Baby/Assassin in Scene 1

FEMALE #4: Lisa Pennington/Dr. Claudia Barber/Lydia Coffee/Angela Goodson

FEMALE #5: Protester 3/Citizen 2/YouTuber/Church Worker 1/Circus Visitor 2/
Church Member 2/Speaker 3

FEMALE #6: Mandy Barlow/Ruth/Circus Visitor 1/Doctor/Townsperson 2/
Rosa Barrett/Church Member 3/Speaker 6

NOTES TO ALL POTENTIAL DIRECTORS:

- This play works best with the fewest number of actors possible. The fifteen-actor breakdown above works much better than adding dozens of actors. Most of the characters are minor and can be played for "type." Having said that, "costume changes" should be minimal, preferably limited to accessories and minor, yet distinct choices.
- The transitions of are of the utmost importance. The scenes have to be played back-to-back, even overlapping if possible. This script is long, but if it is played quickly, with great energy, and with fast-paced, seamless transitions, it can be much shorter that the number of lines indicates. Also, with a proper cutting, it can be performed as a one-act.
- When playing the full-length of the show, please consider placing an intermission between Scenes 42 and 43.
- If possible, as each scene begins, it's best to project the actual names of the scenes on an upstage scrim or cyc. The names can fade away as the scene progresses.

SCENE CHARACTER BREAKDOWN:

Scene 1: Bradford, Jeremiah, Caleb (as bound man), Soldier 1, Soldier 2, Kidnapper, Protester 1, Protester 2, Protester 3, James, Lisa

Scene 2: Citizen 1, Citizen 2

Scene 3: Man 1, Isabel, Caleb, Jeremiah

Scene 4: Citizen 1, Citizen 2

Scene 5: Bradford, Lisa, James

Scene 6: Citizen 1, Citizen 2

Scene 7: Barlow, Eli, Charlie

Scene 8: Citizen 1, Citizen 2

Scene 9: Partygoer 1, Caleb, Betty, Dmitri, Partygoer 2, Announcer, Barker

Scene 10: Bradford, Jeremiah

Scene 11: Actor 1, Late-Night Comedian

Scene 12: Barlow, Charlie

Scene 13: Caleb, Nathan

Scene 14: Actor 1, YouTuber

Scene 15: Eli

Scene 16: Ruth, Lisa, Actor 1

Scene 17: Church Worker 1, Church Worker 2, Isabel, Jeremiah

Scene 18: Speaker 1, Speaker 2, Speaker 3, Speaker 4, Speaker 5, Speaker 6, Speaker 7

Scene 19: Barker, Caleb

Scene 20: Circus Worker 1, Circus Worker 2, Lydia, Visitor 1, Visitor 2, The Child Jeremiah, Montgomery

Scene 21: Bradford

Scene 22: Eli, Angela, Church Member 1, Church Member 2

Scene 23: Betty, Caleb, Dimitri

Scene 24: Abel, Jeremiah

Scene 25: Barlow, Bradford

Scene 26: Barlow, Protester 1, Protester 2, Protester 3, Isabel, Andrea

Scene 27: Teacher

Scene 28: Dmitri, Caleb, Betty, Nathan

Scene 29: Lisa, James, Doctor, Trey, Marshall, Marine

Scene 30: Caleb, Nathan, Man in Towel, Dmitri

Scene 31: Jeremiah

Scene 32: Townsperson 1, Townsperson 2, Protester 1, Protester 2, Caleb, Isabel

Scene 33: Eli

Scene 34: Student

Scene 35: Jeremiah, Michaels, Secret Service Agent 1, Secret Service Agent 2, Actor 1

Scene 36: Dmitri, Betty, Caleb, Jeremiah

Scene 37: Protester 1, Protester 2, Citizen 1, Citizen 2

Scene 38: Teenager 1, Teenager 2, Teenager 3, Frank, Jeremiah (as a teen), Lydia

Scene 39: Donna, Caleb

Scene 40: Isabel, David

Scene 41: David, Donna

Scene 42: David, Jeremiah

Scene 43: Donna, Barker

Scene 44: Betty, Caleb

Scene 45: Jeremiah

Scene 46: James, Bradford

Scene 47: Caleb, Dmitri, Jeremiah, Rosa

Scene 48: Isabel, Jeremiah

Scene 49: Nathan, Dmitri, Caleb, Syrian Man 1, Syrian Man 2

Scene 50: Eli

Scene 51: Nathan, Harold, Tamberol

Scene 52: Nathan, Harold, Jones, Syrian Woman with Baby, Caleb, Kidnapper

Scene 53: Church Member 1, Church Member 2, Church Member 3, Jeremiah

Scene 54: Caleb, Dmitri

Scene 55: Jeremiah, Betty, Isabel, Man 1

Scene 56: Jeremiah, Caleb

Scene 57: Newscaster, Dmitri, Barker, Bradford, Rosa, Jeremiah, James, Donna

Scene 58: Reporter, Eli, Caleb, Jeremiah, Dmitri

DAMASCUS

SCENE I—A THING WITH FEATHERS

Two pulpits are elevated on opposite sides of the stage.

Concentrated lights come up exclusively on the two pulpits as ministers are delivering sermons. In the SR pulpit, we find REVEREND JEREMIAH COFFEE. In the SL pulpit, we find REVEREND JACOB BRADFORD.

BRADFORD & JEREMIAH.   Hope. (*Pause.*) Hope is the reason that I stand before you today:

BRADFORD.   . . . hope that the world will soon change.

JEREMIAH.   . . . hope in a world that will soon change.

BRADFORD & JEREMIAH.   . . . hope in a future,

JEREMIAH.   . . . a future free from the mistakes of the present.

BRADFORD.   . . . a future in which we learn from the mistakes of the present.

Lights come up near the SL pulpit, where we find JAMES and LISA PENNINGTON, in mourning, facing the minister, backs to the audience.

BRADFORD & JEREMIAH.   I truly believe that hope springs eternal,

BRADFORD.   . . . even in days like these.

JEREMIAH.   . . . even in days like these.

A concentrated light comes up on a single chair DL, occupied by a man bound, hooded, alone, seemingly unconscious.

21

Then, a red wash gradually comes up on the entire stage.

During the course of the next few spoken lines, the following happens in slow-motion: two men in US military attire enter UC and, carefully looking around them, rush to the unconscious man, check his vitals, untie him, de-hood him, and carefully begin to take him out the way they entered.

A kidnapper appears DL, shoots one and kills one of the soldiers. The other soldier shoots and kills the kidnapper. Another soldier runs in, gun up. The two soldiers exit, one carrying the unconscious man, the other carrying the body of the fallen soldier.

JEREMIAH.   Samuel Johnson said, "Hope is necessary in every condition." We hold to
            that truth, especially in days like today.

BRADFORD.   Emily Dickinson said, "Hope is a thing with feathers." While no scholar
            has even claimed the market on her meaning, it's obvious that hope is
            elevating, uplifting, powerful, especially in such days of adversity.

JEREMIAH.   Today,

BRADFORD.   Today, we are here under devastating circumstances, yet we still hold
            hope.

JEREMIAH.   . . . we are here in a disturbing time, yet we still hold hope that we can
            change the world around us.

BRADFORD & JEREMIAH.   Let us pray.

As soon as the soldiers leave the stage, protesters silently (but with great energy) enter from SL and SR. They hold signs that say "GOD HATES AMERICA," "THANK GOD FOR DEAD SOLDIERS," and "THE USA DESERVES DAMNATION," etc. (__FOR THE SAKE OF STAGE PRODUCTION, IT MAY BE BETTER IF THE SIGNS ARE ALL BLANK. MAKING THEM BLANK WILL LEAVE MUCH TO THE AUDIENCE'S IMAGINATION, SOMETHING THAT MAY BE EVEN MORE POWERFUL THAN THE PRINTED SIGNS. PERHAPS, THE SIGNS COULD BE GENERIC, SAYING "SIGN OF PROTEST"—TO MAKE A GENERAL POINT.__) They gather around the SL pulpit where BRADFORD and the PENNINGTONS stand.

JEREMIAH.   Father in Heaven, we come to You today in full humility, thanking You
            for the bountiful harvest of love and mercy You have bestowed upon each
            of us.

BRADFORD.   O, Lord, we come into Your presence this day to express our gratitude for
            Your numerous blessings and for the eternal love that You freely give to
            us.

JEREMIAH. We are eternally grateful for the strength You give us and the missions in life on which You kindly send us so that we can fulfill Your purpose.

From SR, we see a shadowy figure which looks remarkably like JEREMIAH COFFEE. He walks in an arc toward C, when an ambiguous figure appears, following him. The first man stops, looks at the SR pulpit. The second figure pulls out a pistol and shoots him. He falls. Immediately, a police officer appears SR and runs up to the fallen man as the ambiguous figure runs UC and then exits UR.

BRADFORD. Thank You, Lord, for giving us direction and purpose, not allowing us to wander aimlessly in the deserts of life, but guiding us with Your protective hand and leading us in the paths You would have us go.

JEREMIAH. Thank you, Lord, for Your hand of justice and wrath that falls upon those who defy Your ways, teaching them lessons.

BRADFORD. Teach us lessons.

JEREMIAH. Teach them lessons.

The protesters begin pumping their signs up and down violently.

PROTESTERS: (*Looking upward*) Teach them!

They freeze.
Lights go to black.

SCENE 2—CITIZENS

CITIZEN 1: We are people. We are citizens. We are keepers.

CITIZEN 2: We are the people, the keepers of thoughts, the keepers of ideas, the keepers of culture, the keepers of posterity.

CITIZEN 1: Mary Shelly: (*holding up large photo of Mary Shelly*)

CITIZEN 2: "Be steady to your purposes and firm as a rock. This ice is not made of such stuff as your hearts may be; it is mutable and cannot withstand you if you say that it shall not."

23

SCENE 3—More Than A Man

When the lights come up, we see ISABEL COFFEE, daughter of JEREMIAH COFFEE, standing with a clipboard. Three "workers" are taking orders from her, dismantling the two pulpit areas from Scene 1.

ISABEL.   Good job, guys. Let's get the stage and the other structures down.

MAN 1.   We'll get it done, Isabel.

ISABEL.   Thanks! We have another rally in Edmonds on Saturday.

A young man, CALEB MARTINEZ, enters, carrying a suitcase. ISABEL does not see him enter.

CALEB.   Isabel Coffee! I'd advise you, Counselor, not to have those men dismantle too many bleachers and stages in one day. You may be sued for workers' comp.

ISABEL.   (*Legitimately excited. Quickly walks to him and hugs him.*) Caleb!

CALEB.   Mom, how are you?

ISABEL.   Much better since you're home. It's been so long since I've seen you.

CALEB.   I know.

The workers transform the set pieces into an abstract structure and exit.

ISABEL.   Your grandfather's going to be delighted that you're home.

CALEB.   The infamous Reverend Dr. Jeremiah Coffee? Happy to see me?

ISABEL.   You know I take offense to the word "infamous," Caleb.

CALEB.   You know it's the accurate description, Counselor.

ISABEL.   I prefer "famous," Counselor.

JEREMIAH.   (*Entering*) Counselor, counselor: is this what I get when my daughter and my grandson both have law degrees—constant talk of "counselors"?

CALEB.   Hello, Counselor. (*Pauses.*) Grandpa.

24

JEREMIAH.   The Infamous Grandpa?

ISABEL.   (*Starting*) Dad . . .

CALEB.   Yes, Grandpa. Infamous. Do you watch the news?

JEREMIAH.   I shape the news. Of course, I watch it. And yes, "infamous" is right.

ISABEL.   It doesn't matter. If we're hated, we're hated. We're doing what we're supposed to be doing.

JEREMIAH.   (*to Caleb*) Why are you here?

CALEB.   Pardon?

JEREMIAH.   Why have you come back?

ISABEL.   To rejoin us!

JEREMIAH.   (*to Caleb*) Counselor? Or shall I say "Thespian"?

CALEB.   (*Pauses*) To see you.

SCENE 4— COMMANDS

CITIZEN 1:   The keepers of words. *(holding sign with "Words" on it)*

CITIZEN 2:   Robert Browning:

CITIZEN 1:   "This grew; I gave commands; Then all smiles stopped together."

SCENE 5—ALL SMILES STOPPED

REVEREND JACOB BRADFORD is standing at a birdcage, feeding his canary. JAMES and LISA PENNINGTON enter.

JAMES.   Reverend Bradford.

25

BRADFORD. James. Lisa. Please, take a seat.

LISA. Thank you.

They sit. BRADFORD sits on the edge of his desk.

BRADFORD. I know you must be going through a torrent of emotions right now. I've never known many people to endure so much as one time.

LISA. It's more than a person can bear.

BRADFORD. I know. And I want you both to know that I'm here to help you with anything that I can.

JAMES. Thank you, Jacob. We may take you up on that.

BRADFORD. I hope you do.

LISA. Nathan couldn't tell us details. He wasn't allowed to. But he did call me to let me know that he was working on a special mission. He wasn't allowed to say when or where or what, but he did call his father and me to let us know, to let us know that he was doing something important and potentially dangerous. I had no idea he would be . . . that he would be . . .

JAMES. That he would be killed by a damned terrorist. (*Pauses.*) Sorry, Jacob.

BRADFORD. No problem. It's accurate.

LISA. You know it's possible, but you don't see it coming directly to you.

BRADFORD. I know.

LISA. And then you delivered such a beautiful sermon at his memorial.

JAMES. You surely did. (*Pauses.*) And then . . .

LISA. And then . . . those people!

JAMES. I don't know if "people" is the proper word. Those animals, those . . .

LISA. James.

JAMES. Those "people" from that perverted church, showing up with their signs of hatred, robbing us of the dignity of our final goodbye to our son.

LISA.   Our Nathan.

BRADFORD. I know. I know. I was as shocked as you. I knew they show up
             everywhere from funerals to parades to museums, spewing their hatred,
             but I honestly wasn't expecting them to come to Nathan's service.

JAMES.   They had no right.

LISA.   It was the funeral for our baby.

JAMES.   They won't get away with it.

BRADFORD. What do you propose?

JAMES.   The first thing: a lawsuit.

BRADFORD. They're on TV all the time, screaming about their First Amendment rights,
             claiming what they do it free speech.

LISA.   That's a blatant abuse.

BRADFORD. I agree, but that's their argument.   That's why I think a lawsuit may not
             work.

JAMES.   That's why there's a second thing.

SCENE 6—WITH FREEDOMS

CITIZEN 2:   With rights come responsibilities. With responsibilities come burdens.
             With burdens come freedoms.

CITIZEN 1:   John Updike: "If you have the guts to be yourself, other people'll pay your
             price." *(holding up sign with dollar sign on it)*

SCENE 7—THE PRICE

MANDY BARLOW. Are you ready, Charlie? This is going to be a fast interview. I
don't know how long we'll get to talk with him, but there are at least
seven big questions I need to ask him.

INTERN. He's here, Ms. Barlow.

BARLOW. Thanks, Cindy.

Eli Connor enters. He is an imposing figure, all confidence, no arrogance.

BARLOW. Mr. Connor!

ELI. Ms. Barlow.

BARLOW. What an honor.

ELI. The pleasure is all mine.

BARLOW. Thank you for taking the time to sit down with us. I know you're a busy
man.

ELI. No problem.

BARLOW. Well, let's get started. Charlie?

CHARLIE. Ready.

BARLOW. Good. (*Pause.*) Good evening, and welcome to *American Spotlight*. I'm
your host, Mandy Barlow, and you're in my light. We are fortunate today
to have snagged an exclusive interview with one of the most formative
voices in cable news today, firebrand journalist and commentator Eli
Connor. His brand of abrasive in-your-face interviews and analysis attracts
viewers from all demographics. Love him or hate him, he tops ratings
night after night with his provocative takes on current events and his
often-confrontational interviews with newsmakers. Although he spends
his nights on *his* side of the desk, tonight we get to ask *him* the tough
questions. Tonight, we welcome Eli Connor. Welcome to American
Spotlight. We're delighted that you agreed to join us.

ELI. Thank you, Mandy. It's good to be here with you.

BARLOW. Mr. Connor?

ELI.   Eli.

BARLOW.   Eli . . . You've been in the business for a long time. What is it about you
           that makes you so divisive, so controversial?

ELI.   I'm not afraid. People don't scare me. Everybody from a pauper to a king
           puts his pants on one leg at a time. The thing is that power corrupts
           people. Some people think they deserve fame and fortune. That's bogus.
           The people are owed the truth about everything that happens.

BARLOW.   The truth?

ELI.   Yeah. The truth.

BARLOW.   And *you* have the truth?

ELI.   Yeah. At least pieces of it. That's my job.

BARLOW.   To be the keeper of the truth?

ELI.   (Pauses.) What's your job?

BARLOW.   To ask questions

ELI.   In order to . . .

BARLOW.   Find answers

ELI.   About?

BARLOW.   The topic at hand. In this case, you.

ELI.   The keeper of the truth?

BARLOW.   Your words, not mine. (*Pauses*) The self-proclaimed savior.

ELI.   Thank you for the opportunity, Ms. Barlow, but this interview is over.

BARLOW.   Wait, Mr. Connor. We've just begun.

ELI.   Funny how life works that way.

BARLOW.   Mr. Connor, my last comment may have been inappropriate. I shouldn't
           have presumed.

ELI.   Well, we both know the adage.

BARLOW.   Mr. Connor, please! I need to ask you about your interview with the President and with Jeremiah Coffee.

ELI.   Have a nice evening, Ms. Barlow.

He exits. She shows frustration with herself.

SCENE 8—GAMES

CITIZEN 2:   The games we play, the people we revere, the ideas we entertain all change us.

CITIZEN 1:   (*Holding up photo of Jack Kerouac*) Jack Kerouac: "The only people for me are the mad ones, the ones who are mad to live, mad to talk, mad to be saved, desirous of everything at the same time, the ones who never yawn or say a commonplace thing, but burn, burn, burn like fabulous yellow roman candles exploding like spiders across the stars."

Citizen 2 holds up photo with stars drawn on it.

SCENE 9—SPIDERS ACROSS THE STARS

A formal masquerade.
Several partygoers in costumes and masks. Classical music.
Some people talk, some dance.
CALEB enters in costume.

PARTYGOER 1: Hello.

CALEB.   Hello.

BETTY.   I'd know that walk anywhere.

CALEB.   I'm in disguise. You don't know who I am.

BETTY.   Oh, shut up, Caleb.

DMITRI.   (*In thick Russian accent*) Caleb, I am so glad that you find yourself here. (*Caleb, in frustration in being recognized, takes off his mask to examine it to see if it's transparent.*) What an amazing masquerade party! Joanne told me you and she greatly planned this escapade. Bravo.

BETTY.   Everybody's loving it, but they aren't crazy about the music.

CALEB.   It's authentic.

BETTY.   Too much so.

CALEB.   It's called ambiance.

DMITRI.   What is that?

BETTY.   Auditory boredom.

CALEB.   Atmosphere.

PARTYGOER 2: Excellent masquerade, Mr. Martinez. The university law council has never seen a social event quite like this.

CALEB.   I figured we could stand a little class. There are only so many animal house parties a person can abide without wanting a little change.

PARTYGOER 2: Well, I don't know if everyone agrees with you, but I certainly do. And so does Professor Barker.

BETTY.   Dr. Barker's here?

PARTYGOER 2: Yes, she is. And she said something about wanting to talk with you.

ANNOUNCER. It's time for the first official dance of the evening. If everyone who took your proper lessons would get into position, we will begin.

The dance begins, and everyone on stage participates in the minuet. As the dance proceeds, one person (Dr. Claudia Barker) pulls Caleb out of the line and brings him downstage. The dance continues in slow motion and with muted sound behind them.

31

CALEB.   I'm sorry, but this is my party, and I have to stay in the . . . (*She pulls her mask off, revealing her identity.*) Oh, Professor Barker. I had no idea it was you.

BARKER.   Of course, you didn't.

CALEB.   I'm pleased that you chose to come tonight.

BARKER.   I don't miss a chance to wear a mask. I teach law, remember?

CALEB.   I understand.

BARKER.   I appreciate your throwing this masque for the current law students. It's good for them to see an alumnus taking interest in the old alma mater.

CALEB.   Always, Professor.

BARKER.   And speaking of masques, Mr. Martinez, we not only dance at them, we also wear them, don't we?

CALEB.   I don't follow.

BARKER.   I can't believe in all the years you studied at YLS, you kept the secret of your parentage from us.

CALEB.   Oh.

BARKER.   In a million years, I never would have placed you as the grandson of the Reverend Jeremiah Coffee.

CALEB.   That makes two of us. Well, with my mom, three.

BARKER.   So, your mom must be Isabel Coffee.

CALEB.   The one and only.

BARKER.   Both of them graduate of this school, and not a word.

CALEB.   It's not exactly a legacy that the vast majority would embrace.

BARKER.   Nonetheless, I know your family must be proud that you followed in the YLS footsteps.

CALEB.   Elated.

BARKER.   You sound less than.

CALEB.   I did what I had to do, and I think I proved myself on my own terms.

BARKER.   And what does the grand old preacher think about your new foray?

CALEB.   I think he is more than happy that I've opened up my law office.

BARKER.   I'm not talking about law, Caleb.

CALEB.   What?

BARKER.   What does Jeremiah Coffee think about his lawyer grandson becoming an actor?

CALEB.   Professor Barker . . .

DMITRI.   Caleb, I wanted to see if . . . Oh, Professor Barker. I'm sorry.

BARKER.   It's okay, Mr. Kovalenko. We're just about done here.

BETTY.   Dmitri, did you find . . . Oh, Dr. Barker.

BARKER.   Good evening, Ms. Trevino.

BETTY.   We didn't mean to interrupt.

BARKER.   No worries. Caleb and I were just about to take a little walk. I have a little project to discuss with him. Excuse us.

CALEB.   Excuse us.

They walk offstage together.

BETTY.   I wonder what that's about?

DMITRI.   Maybe she is what you call a tiger.

BETTY.   A tiger?

DMITRI.   You know, a woman who is older and desires the love of a younger man.

BETTY.   A cougar.

DIMITRI.   That's what I said.   Maybe that's what the professor is.

BETTY.   I have a feeling that it's more than that.

33

DMITRI.   I don't know. The romance is a strong force. I know from experience.

BETTY.   Something's up with Caleb. He looked nervous. And I'm going to find out why.

SCENE 10—FUNDAMENTALLY

BRADFORD. One must never forget that fundamentally, God feels immense love for us.

JEREMIAH.   One must never forget that fundamentally, God feels immense hatred for us.

BRADFORD. We live in difficult days, but we know in the midst of adversity that we have a benevolent God, looking out of us, granting us grace, showing us favor. Let us all pray for peace. Thank you for watching this week. Visit us daily for insight and encouragement.

JEREMIAH.   Yes, I said hatred. There is a major misinterpretation, a pie-in-the-sky, when-you-wish-upon-a star caricature of the Almighty. People so long for a God made in their own image that they make one to suit their needs. The great irony is that their gold calf is not in their own image. The image of man is not pleasant. He is a profound stench upon the planet. And God knows man and smells the vulgarity of his ways. Yes, God hates mankind, and He hates America. Yes, God hates America. This country is vile and despicable. We live selfish lives. Sex is everywhere. Intoxication is the norm. Our churches are grotesque. Our leaders are sons of Satan. We embrace homosexuality. We own more guns than we do Bibles. We stick our noses in the business of other nations. We treat every group and every person as equals with each other. We're dying because God has ordained it so. Soldiers dying. AIDS. Children's diseases. Urban violence. Political strife. National debt. Everything that this nation deserves because plain and simple: God hates America. And it's our job to voice this point of view. Yes, it's an unpopular point of view, but I was never called to be popular. I was called to speak the truth. I send out the truth. That's why we attend important events, funerals, meetings, to speak the truth. And we will continue to do so.

SCENE 11: WHAT THE NIGHT HOLDS

Music from a late-night talk show. Laughter from a studio audience. A random actor holds a large sign that says "THE LATE SHOW LIVE WITH TERRY TY."

LATE-NIGHT COMEDIAN. In other news, controversial journalist Eli Connor recently interviewed controversial hate monger Jeremiah Coffee. (*Audience boos.*) In the interview, Coffee supposedly explains why he and his church group protest at soldiers' funerals and other venues and why he generally hates everyone and everything. When asked by Connor why he hates so much, he answered that he suffers from severe social allergies, specifically "gay" fever. (*Audience breaks out in laughter.*) When the interview was over, he morphed back into himself, but funny thing is he looked the same. (*Audience laughs even more.*)

SCENE 12: JUST LIKE YOU

BARLOW. True vulnerability happens when we don't know what we're doing. We say things and do things to been seen and heard and realize that we've crossed a line or burned a bridge.

CHARLIE. (*holding camera*) But facing those things makes us stronger, more willing to be ourselves not only in front of others but to ourselves.

BARLOW. But we need to be honest enough to need someone and to be honest with them. (*She takes Charlie's hand. They look at each other.*)

CHARLIE. A real friend is someone who knows the song in your heart and can sing it back to you when you have forgotten the words.

BARLOW. That's sweet.

CHARLIE. Just like you.

SCENE 13: FORGOTTEN THE WORDS

A law school study group is finishing its session. Caleb is leading it.

CALEB. And that, ladies and gentlemen, ends our group session for this evening. I feel that we had a productive meeting. I'll take the notes to Dr. Barker first thing in the morning. You all are going to make amazing attorneys. I appreciate your attendance, and I'm particularly impressed with the new members of our cadre. Have a great evening. Before you hit the pubs, remember that most of you have an exam first thing in the morning.

The members start to disperse.

NATHAN. Caleb?

CALEB. Yes?

NATHAN. I'm Nathan Pennington, one of the newbies here tonight.

CALEB. I know. The professor mentioned that you'd be attending.

NATHAN. She said that she had set me up for success or failure, that the outcome would be up to me.

CALEB. It always is. Don't worry. You'll do fine. This is just her way of making sure the best and the brightest don't stagnate in the cesspool of corporate law.

NATHAN. Ah, I try to avoid those cesspools.

CALEB. Why are you at Yale Law then?

NATHAN. (*Taken aback a little*) Well . . .

CALEB. A joke. It was a joke.

NATHAN. I was hoping.

CALEB. So, Nathan. What are your plans after you get out of the grinder?

NATHAN. Well, it's not very typical for your typical law student.

CALEB. I don't fit well with "typical," so try me.

NATHAN.   I'm a Marine. After I finish here, I'm requesting a run in special forces.

CALEB.   Really?

NATHAN.   Really. That doesn't hurt my standing in Barker's X-Men, does it?

CALEB.   Well, I can't speak for Dr. Barker, but it does nothing but increase your standing in my eyes.

NATHAN.   Thanks. I want to do as much as I can and serve as much as I can in every way that I can.

CALEB.   Bloody hell! You're an idealist—an idealist wannabe lawyer. With a gun. Who let the oxymorons loose?

NATHAN.   (*Laughing*) That would be me.

CALEB.   Come on, Mr. Smith. Let's go get a drink.

NATHAN.   I have an exam in the morning.

CALEB.   I have the answer key.

They leave.

SCENE 14: FEEDING THE 5000

A passing actor holds us a sign that says "SOCIAL MEDIA 101."

YOUTUBER. Yo, yo, yo! Hello, subscribers! Thanks for bumping me up over 5,000! It happened last night around 11 p.m. We were three away about 10:30, and when I looked a few minutes later, we'd gone over. I love you guys! You are the bestest of the bestest. I know I'm crazy and wild and funny, and it's so cool to know that you know it, too! You're the best friends a girl could ever ask for! We're going to talk fashion and gingers today, the two best topics in the world. Remember that we're following all the crap that's happening in the world, too, so if you have crap you're putting up with, I want to hear from you. I just love crap! (*Takes out her cell phone*) Wait a minute! Real-time alert on the cell phone! You heard it right here! There's some military attack somewhere on the other side of the world. Hey, hey. You guys be careful over there! Stay safe. Anyway, it's ginger time!

SCENE 15: RIGHT HERE

Broadcast news music blares. Eli Connor, in a suit, is sitting at his desk. As the music subsides, Connor begins.

ELI.   Good evening, I'm Eli Connor, and you're watching Eye on the World, where we look where we're not supposed to look so you can know the truth around you. There's a lot going on on the planet tonight, so we need to get started. Today's opening statement: Crisis in the Middle East. Today, forces hostile to the Syrian government seized the eastern sections of Damascus, the oldest continuously inhabited city in the world. The Syrian government issued a statement at 6 p.m. tonight asking for assistance from the international community.

SCENE 16: CROSSING PATHS

Lisa Pennington crosses with a purse and shopping bag. Another woman, purse in hand, sees her and speaks.

RUTH. Lisa? Lisa Pennington?

LISA.   Yes. Ruth? Is that you?

RUTH. Yes! Lisa, it's good to see you. (*They hug.*) How are you?

LISA.   I'm good. Everything's good. Just super busy with everything.

RUTH. I won't keep you then.

LISA.   Oh, I didn't mean *that*. (*Laughs*) I'm just saying that life's busy.

RUTH. Oh, I know. For us, too. James still at Franklin and Marshall?

LISA.   Actually, no. About six months ago, he got a job offer from Ranford, Berry, and Peterson.

RUTH. That's great, Lisa. That's pretty impressive.

LISA.   I'm proud of him.

RUTH. As well you should be. How's your practice?

LISA.   All teeth, all day. Screaming kids. Did I mention teeth?

RUTH.   (*Laughing*) Believe me. I know. Me, too. That's why we went to dental
             school, right?

LISA.   And paid dearly for it. Oh, Rachel is expecting! She's due any day!

RUTH.   Oh, Lisa. Congrats! I haven't seen her since the wedding. I know you're
             excited.

LISA.   I am. James is beside himself—with the first grandbaby and with Nathan
             finally finishing law school, in between his excursions into war zones.

RUTH.   War zones?

LISA.   He rejoined, simultaneously. Twice. Freedoms. He lives and breathes
             "guaranteeing freedoms." He's no hypocrite.

An actor enters, holding a large photograph of GEORGE WASHINGTON.

ACTOR 1.   If freedom of speech is taken away, then dumb and silent we may be led,
             like sheep to the slaughter.

SCENE 17: SHEEP TO THE SLAUGHTER

CHURCH WORKER 1. Do you have any more sign handles?

CHURCH WORKER 2. They're over by the door. You'll have to open a new box.

CHURCH WORKER 1. Okay.

CHURCH WORKER 2. Could you bring me some of those fasteners by the shelf?

ISABEL.   (*Entering*) How's it going?

CHURCH WORKER 1. It's going well. We're finishing up the last batch of 100 now.
             These are pretty straightforward.

ISABEL.   Good. They need to be. (*Picking them up to look at them one by one*)
             Concise. Direct. Cutting. Making people think.

39

CHURCH WORKER 2. Not that it does any good.

ISABEL.   How so?

CHURCH WORKER 2. You know what I mean. They come to see what we're doing.
             If doesn't make them change. They just get angry with us.   They're blind
             to the truth.

ISABEL.   But we still proclaim it. And you're right. None of them will ever get it.
             It's just us. We're the only ones. The only ones. That narrow path may
             hold only seventy or eighty, but that's alright. We know. We know.

CHURCH WORKER 1. We know.

ISABEL.   That wicked constitution that allows for every kind of evil and perversion
             also allows us to speak our minds how we see fit, and if they don't want to
             hear it, they have no choice, because we're going to say it and say it loud
             and in their faces.

CHURCH WORKER 1. And they say that they have the right to do as they wish.

ISABEL.   Well, people have the "right" to sin, but they are going to burn forever in a
             lake of endless torment for their deeds. And it's our job to tell them
             what's on their ticket stub.

CHURCH WORKER 1: Hallelujah!

JEREMIAH.   *(Entering.)* You've hit upon the essence of the truth, Isabel.

ISABEL.   Dad! We were just talking about the beauty of the first amendment.

JEREMIAH.   The right to be right.

CHURCH WORKER 1. Right!

CHURCH WORKER 2. And those others have the right to be wrong.

JEREMIAH.   Indeed. Indeed, they do. And indeed, they are. But the payday is coming,
             and it's coming soon.

ISABEL.   Very soon.

JEREMIAH.   *(Lifting up the signs and reading them.)* God Hates Soldiers. God Hates
             America. Thank God for Dead Soldiers. God Hates the Perverts. God
             Hates You.   Yes, this is a fine batch. We should be just about ready.

SCENE 18: TOLERANCE?

ACTOR 2 walks out to the center of the stage and holds a large sign that says "TOLLERANCE?"—then walks offstage so that the next actors can enter.

One by one, several people move downstage: (SPEAKER 1) an effeminate man, (SPEAKER 2) a hunter, wearing camouflage, (SPEAKER 3) a tattooed, "emo" young woman, (SPEAKER 4) an older white man in a suit, (SPEAKER 5) a man dressed in traditional Arab clothes, (SPEAKER 6) a youth dressed in street garb (hoody, etc.), (SPEAKER 7) a college professor.

1.	You look at me and decide that you don't like me.
4.	You see how I dress and hear how I talk, and you hate me.
6.	You hate me for who I am.
2.	You hate me for what I do.
5.	You hate me for what I teach.
7.	You hate me for what I teach.
3.	You hate me for how I look.
1., 3. 7.	You do think I'm going to tell you how you are wrong?
2., 6.	How we should all love each other and not judge?
4., 5.	How we should be tolerant of each other?
1., 2., 3., 4., 5., 6., 7.	Tolerance?
1.	I demand tolerance of you.
5.	I demand tolerance of you.
2.	I demand tolerance of you.
1., 2., 3., 4., 5., 6., 7.	But
1., 3., 5., 7.	. . . it'll be a cold day in hell

2., 4. 6.   . . . before I accept you.

1., 2., 3., 4., 5., 6., 7. I'm disgusted by who you are and what you stand for.

3.   And you can mark my words.

1., 2., 3., 4., 5., 6., 7. I will fight with every part of my being to make sure that you not
only accept who and what I am, but embrace and celebrate it. Your
current opinion is not acceptable. You will change, and you will shed
your dangerous views. My freedom to be who I am is more important
than your freedom of speech.

SCENE 19: IT'S WHAT WE DO, RIGHT?

Dr. Claudia Barker's Yale Law School office

BARKER.   Caleb, can I get you a cup of tea?

CALEB.   No, thank you. I'm fine.

BARKER.   Look, you're one of the best minds and most talented students to come
through here in years.   Let me cut to the chase.

CALEB.   Thank you, and okay.

BARKER.   My dissertation for my doctorate was about the importance of freedom
and the pursuit of justice.

CALEB.   I know. I read it.

BARKER.   You did?

CALEB.   Every word. Twice.

BARKER.   All right. Good. That interesting, huh?

CALEB.   Spellbinding.

BARKER.   You're not in my class anymore. You don't have to kiss up.

CALEB.   Old habits. (*Smiles*)

BARKER.   Justice is very important to me. Very important. I have something I need
            to tell you. I wish I had all the details, but I don't, and I hope that you can
            piece the puzzle together.

CALEB.   Okay.

BARKER.   People's lives depend upon it. Justice depends upon it. And strangely
            enough, freedom itself depends upon it.

CALEB.   Dr. Barker, what is it?

BARKER.   Your grandfather is a man who can cause many people quite a bit of
            heartache.

CALEB.   I know.

BARKER.   And it's not your fault. I'm just telling you because it's much deeper than
            you think. He has not only hurt lives with his hatred and his rhetoric, but
            I'm afraid that there are more sinister things that he's been responsible for
            and sadly some things that he is currently doing.

CALEB.   I didn't know you were so knowledgeable about my grandfather.

BARKER.   I am. And there is a reason. Caleb, things are much worse than you think.
            I need to find a lady named Donna. I knew her as Donna McDaniel. In
            fact, she was my cousin. I grew up in Oklahoma City, and she grew up in
            western Kansas. Then she married a man named Joe, Joe Martinez.

CALEB.   What?

BARKER.   I need you to find Donna Martinez. She is your grandmother. She is
            alive. And there are things she knows that you need to find out and fix.
            Then, if you're willing, I need you to go to Denver. There are wrongs to
            be righted. That's what we do, isn't it?

SCENE 20: LIONS, TIGERS, . . .

The sounds of the circus are everywhere. People walk by eating popcorn, laughing. It is obvious that it's many years in the past. LYDIA COFFEE and her young son, JEREMIAH enter. Young Jeremiah is in awe.

CIRCUS WORKER 2 walks out holding a large sign that says "LIONS AND TIGERS AND BEARS"—and passes on by through the crowd.

LYDIA.   Here we are, Jeremiah.   Just like you wanted.

CIRCUS WORKER 1. Gather round, one and all! Gather round. (*People, young and old begin to gather*) Welcome, citizens of the fair city of Damascus, Kansas. Welcome to the Finley and Fordham Circus, the biggest traveling circus in the American heartland.

VISITOR 1.   You have elephants?

CIRCUS WORKER 1. Do we have elephants?

VISITOR 1.   Well, do you?

CIRCUS WORKER 1. We have not one, not two, but three large African elephants!

Everyone claps.

VISITOR 2.   What about lions?

CIRCUS WORKER 1. Do we have lions?

VISITOR 2.   Do you, Mister?

CIRCUS WORKER 1. Of course, we do, or my name's not Nigel Finiggleworth.

VISITOR 2.   How many?

CIRCUS WORKER 1. Well, it's more than five and less than seven!

CHILD JEREMIAH. That would be six!

CIRCUS WORKER 1. That's right, young man. You are right. Six. Six ferocious, man-eating lions.

LYDIA.   Don't scare him.

44

CHILD JEREMIAH. I'm not scared!

LYDIA.   Just be careful. He's a child.

CHILD JEREMIAH. I'm not a baby.

VISITOR 1.   What about clowns? Have any of those?

CIRCUS WORKER 1. The happiest, friendliest clowns on the whole planet.

VISITOR 1.   Clowns are good.

CIRCUS WORKER 1. (to himself) Generally.

VISITOR 2.   That's saying a lot, Mister. This is a big planet.

CIRCUS WORKER 1. Not that big. By 1980, man'll be able to fly around the whole
        thing in less than an hour.

VISITOR 2.   Bologna!

CIRCUS WORKER 1. Watch your language, sir! This is a family affair.

VISITOR 2.   Sounds like something else to me. Sounds like a big scam.

CIRCUS WORKER 1. Sir!

VISITOR 2.   I bet you don't even have any animals at all!

*A series of screams ensue from SL. The sound of fearful crowds, elephants, lions, etc. on
the loose. People run from SL yelling, "Watch out! The animals are out!" and "They let
the animals out."*

VISITOR 2.   (*Looks SL. Then looks at Circus Worker*). So you do. (*Then he runs full
        speed SR.*)

CIRCUS WORKER 1. Everybody! Run for your lives. They can be vicious! (*He runs
        SR.*)

*The other patrons run off stage. Lydia pulls Young Jeremiah SR, trying to escape, but he
breaks free and walks slowly CR, looking SL. Lydia tries to pull at him but to no avail.
An imposing figure of a man wearing a suit walks in slowly from SL. He (RC
Montgomery) walks straight toward the Young Jeremiah. Then he veers slightly DL.*)

MONTGOMERY. Head on home, everybody! Head on home where you belong. This no place for fine Christian people. It's no place for any people. Go home. There's no pleasure in anything but the church. Everything else is sin. This is the devil's playground. No pleasure in life in anything. God's creatures have been set free! No gazing at animals, no gambling games of ball tossing, no ungodly bearded women bound for the torments, no perverted house of mirrors, no sports, no performance, no idol pleasures. Come this Sunday to find out the only way, the only congregation bound for Glory, the real straight and narrow: Damascus's only Elect Church led by yours truly, the Reverend RC Montgomery.

The whole time, Young Jeremiah and eventually Lydia have listened to Montgomery in awe. Montgomery turns to look at Jeremiah.

MONTOGOMERY. And what have we here? Not running away, young man?

YOUNG JEREMIAH. No.

LYDIA.   "No, sir," Jeremiah.

MONTGOMERY. It's all right. Not scared, young man?

YOUNG JEREMIAH. No.

MONTGOMERY. There are wild animals on the loose.

YOUNG JEREMIAH. I don't care.

MONTGOMERY. Are you scared of me?

YOUNG JEREMIAH. No.

LYDIA. Jeremiah! *(almost scolding for being so casual)*

MONTGOMERY. What's your name, young man? Is it Jeremiah?

YOUNG JEREMIAH. Jeremiah Monroe Coffee.

MONTGOMERY. Jeremiah Monroe Coffee. That's quite a name, young man. It has a ring to it. Big things are in store for you. God has a task for you to accomplish.

YOUNG JEREMIAH. I know.

MONTGOMERY. Do you, now?

YOUNG JEREMIAH. Yes.

MONTGOMERY. And it won't make you beloved among men.

YOUNG JEREMIAH. Good.

MONTGOMERY. Come with me. We have a lot to talk about.

LYDIA.   But?

MONTGOMERY. You too, mother.   We'll go start our own feast while we talk.

They exit SR. YOUNG JEREMIAH and MONTGOMERY walk with purpose, side by side. LYDIA follows in a daze. The sounds of the animals subside.

SCENE 21: THUS SAITH

BRADFORD. (*in his pulpit*) Ladies and gentlemen, thank you for your attendance this morning and for your lovely singing. It does my heart good to hear voices raised in beautiful harmony for the purpose of praise. If you'll turn to our second scripture reading this morning, we'll be looking at the Book of Isaiah, Chapter 17:

The burden of Damascus. Behold, Damascus is taken away from being a city, and it shall be a ruinous heap. The cities of Aroer are forsaken: they shall be for flocks, which shall lie down, and none shall make them afraid. The fortress also shall cease from Ephraim, and the kingdom from Damascus, and the remnant of Syria: they shall be as the glory of the children of Israel, saith the Lord of hosts. And in that day it shall come to pass, that the glory of Jacob shall be made thin, and the fatness of his flesh shall wax lean. And it shall be as when the harvestman gathereth the corn, and reapeth the ears with his arm; and it shall be as he that gathereth ears in the valley of Rephaim.

Thus saith the Lord. Thus saith his shepherd. Amen.

SCENE 22: NEVER AGAIN

Newscaster music. ELI CONNER is on the air.

ELI.   And we are back. Welcome to continuing breaking news. As we reported
                    earlier, forces hostile to the government of Syria have taken not only the
                    eastern half of the city of Damascus, but are well on their way to
                    swallowing up all sections except for the heart of government. These
                    rebel armies have moved unimpeded across the nation and have waltzed
                    into the backyard of international intrigue and power. Jordan, Saudi
                    Arabia, and Israel have all put their people on high alert, readying their
                    own forces and preparing shelters for worst-case scenarios. It's one thing
                    to have a rogue dictator. It's another to have a terrorist group with no
                    limits taking over a major nation. We'd better wake up. Instead, we focus
                    on other things, stupid things happening here. The rest of the world is
                    burning, and we have idiots on the streets protesting at the National
                    Holocaust Museum. You heard me right. Members of the infamous Elect
                    Street Church out of Denver, Colorado have made their way again to
                    headlines and to the hatred of other Americans as they protest outside of
                    the National Holocaust Museum, holding up anti-Semitic signs and
                    harassing bypassers.

*Protesters enter DL holding up signs: God Hates Jews, The Jews Killed Jesus, There's a
New Chosen People.*

ELI.   We've sent out our roving correspondent, Angela Goodson, to investigate
                    and ask a few questions. Angela?

ANGELA.   Thank you, Eli. We're at the National Holocaust Museum at the
                    beginning of the Jewish Sabbath to witness a protest of Elect Street
                    Church, whose leader is the well-known Jeremiah Coffee. Why they
                    protest here and why now we do not know. The church has a history of
                    showing up at funerals of soldiers, at government events, at major
                    speeches, at graduations, at weddings of famous Americans, at wakes for
                    known homosexuals, and at college sports events. But this time, they
                    have chosen the American Holocaust Museum, and we're about to ask
                    why. Ma'am. Excuse me, ma'am.

CHURCH MEMBER 1. Yes?

ANGELA: We can't help but notice that you're protesting at the American Holocaust
                    Museum.

CHURCH MEMBER 1. I hope you can notice. Otherwise, you'd be as blind literally as
                    you are figuratively.

ANGELA.   Okay. Why are you here?

CHURCH MEMBER 1. To protest. It's our first-amendment right and duty to speak our minds and tell the truth.

ANGELA.   And what exactly are you saying here?

CHURCH MEMBER 1. Aren't our signs clear?

ANGELA.   What do you have against the Jewish people?

CHURCH MEMBER 1. Against them? Against them? Nothing. We have nothing against them. It's just that God hates them like He hates the rest of you. They think they are still the chosen people of God, but they forfeited that right when they killed Jesus, when they hung Him on the cross.

ANGELA.   So, you are protesting that the Jewish people killed Jesus over 2000 years ago.

CHURCH MEMBER 1. Yeah. And that God hates them for it.

ANGELA.   But you're here at the National . . .

CHURCH MEMBER 2. Something that didn't happen. Couldn't have happened.

ANGELA.   The Holocaust?

CHURCH MEMBER 2. Yeah.

ANGELA.   But there's a ton of historical proof that . . .

CHURCH MEMBER 2. Proof? Doctored. But even if it did happen, so what? Payback is tough for killing God Himself. People get what they deserve.

ANGELA.   But wasn't Jesus a man who taught the beauty and power of love and forgiveness?

CHURCH MEMBER 2. There you go with that phony narrative. God is a God of wrath and vengeance. He will have no mercy on mankind.

ANGELA.   But the Bible says . . .

CHURCH MEMBER 1. That Bible you read has been doctored up to, to say what people want it to say, not what God actually said.

49

ANGELA.   So, you come to protest at the museum and harass people?

CHURCH MEMBER 2. We haven't touched a soul. We have stood here with our signs.
                 People have yelled and spit at us, and yes, we respond. We have a right to
                 protest and to respond to people's verbal attacks, right?

ANGELA.   You've stood here on one of the busiest streets . . .

CHURCH MEMBER 2. We have that right, right?

ANGELA.   (*Ignoring the question*) You have a reputation for inciting anger as you
            mock soldiers, America in general, gays, teachers, other ministers, almost
            anyone who doesn't see life your way.

CHURCH MEMBER 2. Was there a question there?

ANGELA.   Does it bother you that your brand of hatred causes so much frustration
            and pain for so many people?

CHURCH MEMBER 1. Does it *bother* us?

ANGELA.   Yes?

CHURCH MEMBER 2. We thank God for it.

SCENE 23: THE GREAT WHITE WAY

*ACTOR 2 quickly walks across stage holding a sign saying "THE GREAT WHITE
WAY"—looking around in awe, then running off.*
*Caleb walks, eating a candy bar, backpack over his shoulder. Betty enters, followed by
Dmitri.*

BETTY.   Caleb!

CALEB.   (*Stopping*) Yeah?

BETTY.   "Yeah"?

CALEB.   Sorry, Betty. My mind's a million miles away.

BETTY.   Well, of course it is. Congratulations!

CALEB.   Thank you.

DMITRI.   Yes, congratulations!

CALEB.   Thank you, and congrats to you two as well.

BETTY.   Thank *you*, but *we* didn't get a major role in a Broadway revival of an American classic!

CALEB.   You're in the production.

DMITRI.   But "John Proctor" won't be beside my name in the Playbill.

CALEB.   We're all blessed.

BETTY.   But some are luckier than others.

CALEB.   Blessed.

DMITRI.   How about happy? (*Does a happy dance*)

BETTY.   Dmitri, in public? Really?

DMITRI.   I am an actor. I am paid to look foolish.

BETTY.   You need a raise.

Caleb laughs.

DMITRI.   Wait. Was that an insult?

BETTY.   To you? Never! You're the best and strangest friend I've ever had.

DMITRI.   Thank you?

BETTY.   (*to Caleb, touches him on the arm*) And I owe you thanks for last night. That was the best time I've had a dinner in a long time. It was nice to just relax.

CALEB.   I'm glad you enjoyed it. I had a good time, too.

DMITRI.   Caleb and Betty sitting in a tree . . .

BETTY.   Dmitri!

DMITRI.   K-I-S-S-I-N-G!

BETTY.   Dmitri!

DMITRI.   First comes love, then comes the carriage of the baby . . .

CALEB.   Dmitri.

DMITRI.   Then comes . . .

BETTY.   Please!

DMITRI.   Wait. I got that mixed up.

CALEB.   Yes, you did.

DMITRI.   Baby? Well, not really? Not today! (*Laughs*)

BETTY.   Are you five years old?

DMITRI.   I was born on Leap Day, so yes. (*Laughs*)

BETTY.   Please don't ruin potentially good things.

CALEB.   (*Smiling*) He's not ruining anything. It's okay. Really.

BETTY.   Okay. It's just so hard, especially in this city, you know?

CALEB.   I know.

BETTY.   With all the crazy people.

CALEB.   I know.

BETTY.   And you like someone, and he's on meth or some other mind-altering
           substance that makes his teeth look like a trash heap.

CALEB.   I know.

BETTY.   And you like someone else, and he is so much of a corporate type that he
           hates the theatre and sees it as a waste of time. Boring!

CALEB.   I know.

BETTY.   And then you find someone who is genuinely nice and who shares your
           interests and he is either mentally ill or nine times out of ten he's gay. Oh,
           please tell me you're not gay.

CALEB.   I'm not gay.

BETTY.   Are you sure?

CALEB.   Positive.

BETTY.   Have you checked?

CALEB.   Checked what?

BETTY.   Whatever it is in a man that tells him that he bats for the boys' team?

CALEB.   Betty, I don't have a switch or an indicator. I just know who I am.

DMITRI.   Forty percent of men in straight relationships act out of internal feelings for their male friends?

BETTY.   Dmitri! Why would say that?

DMITRI.   It's reality, Betty!

BETTY.   Forty percent?

DMITRI.   Well, I made that part up, but you get my point.

BETTY.   Dmitri. Just be your happy self.

DMITRI.   (*Singing*) 'Cause I'm happy!!!

BETTY.   (*to Caleb*) You're going to be the best John Proctor this city has seen in generations.

CALEB.   You're too kind.

BETTY.   I mean, a lawyer. Who in their right mind would expect a Yale Law graduate to want a part in a Broadway production, much less land one.

CALEB.   I'm a strange bird.

DMITRI.   Yes, you are. But I like you.

CALEB.   Thank you, Dmitri.

DMITRI.   And I'm in the production, too. A revival of a classic. But I have to be going. I'm auditioning today for a role in Lee Lawson's new show this fall!

BETTY.   Seriously?

CALEB.   Dmitri, his plays are awful. The same stories, the same style, over and over.

DMITRI.   But it's Lee Lawson!

CALEB.   His plays aren't good.

DMITRI.   I know, but the critics love everything he does.

BETTY.   His cast could step out on stage and just stare and the audience and leave, and he'd get excellent reviews.

CALEB.   Why?

DMITRI.   Because he's Lee Lawson.

BETTY.   The critics are scared to death to be honest about his work. He's so loved that if one critic dared to speak the truth or dared not to praise him, they'd be blackballed. It's happened before. They loose credibility.

CALEB.   That is so unfair.

DMITRI.   But he's Lee Lawson. He's such a nice guy, too.

BETTY.   Go to your audition, Dmitri.

DMITRI.   If I get it, it'll look great on my vita. I mean . . . Lee Lawson.

CALEB.   I think I've got into the wrong business.

BETTY.   No. You're great at this. It's just a crazy network of ego strokers.

DMITRI.   Have a great afternoon, guys. I have to go stand for Lee.

BETTY.   Don't act too well. You won't get the part.

DMITRI.   Okay? (*Leaves*)

CALEB.   Want to get some lunch?

BETTY.   That's the way to ask for a proper date in New York City. Let's go.

They exit.

SCENE 24: JUST LEAVE

ABEL MONTOGOMERY, age 19, sits on a stump, whittling on a piece of wood. With his every word and movement, it's obvious that he is self-confident and aware of his own beauty. A sixteen-year-old JEREMIAH COFFEE runs up and stops.

ABEL.   There you are, Jeremiah Coffee.

JEREMIAH. Hey!

ABEL.   You ask me to meet you here, and you're late.

JEREMIAH. I'm sorry. Your dad had me busy working on a lot of things for the church. I tried to leave twice, but each time he stopped me and asked me to do more. What could I do? Say "No, Brother Montgomery, sir. I can't help you?" No, I couldn't. Not your dad.

ABEL.   You could have told him you were meeting me.

JEREMIAH. No.

ABEL.   Why not?

JEREMIAH. I don't know. I just . . . I don't know.

ABEL.   You're a crazy bird, Jeremiah.

JEREMIAH. There's no need to be mean, Abel!

ABEL.   Stop wearing your feelings on your sleeve. I'm picking with you.

JEREMIAH. Oh.

ABEL.   So, why'd you send word to meet me out here?

JEREMIAH. (*his mind elsewhere*) What?

ABEL.   Jeremiah Coffee, why did you want me to meet you way out here? What's up?

JEREMIAH. Oh, nothing. I just thought we could talk about things. You know, like we did a few weeks ago. I don't know.

ABEL.   Well, okay. But out here?

JEREMIAH.   I don't know, Abel. I thought maybe you could tell me about things. Maybe we could go fishing?

ABEL.   You don't have many friends, do you?

JEREMIAH.   What's that supposed to mean?

ABEL.   Don't take it as an insult. But it's true, isn't it?

JEREMIAH.   What?

ABEL.   That you don't have many friends.

JEREMIAH.   I don't need friends really. Your father says that when the men of the world like you, you're doing something wrong. We have to be steadfast for right in the face of the enemy. The world is going to hell.

ABEL.   That sounds just like my father.

JEREMIAH.   RC Montgomery is a good man!

ABEL.   I have no doubt about that, Jeremiah. I guess he's happy to see someone taking after him, even if it's not his own flesh and blood.

JEREMIAH.   He's been good to me. My own father left when I was little. Your father has treated me like a son.

ABEL.   I know.

JEREMIAH.   He's good.

ABEL.   I said I know. But you need friends, Jeremiah. You need people close to your own age you can talk with, depend upon.

JEREMIAH.   That's why I was hoping that you could . . . we could talk and . . . you know, be . . . friends.

ABEL.   I know.

JEREMIAH.   I mean . . .

ABEL.   It's all good. We can be friends.

JEREMIAH.   *(After an awkward pause)* So, what's been happening with you?

ABEL.   (*Laughs*) With me? Well. I've been trying to work.

JEREMIAH.   Yeah. At the grocery store!

ABEL.   Yeah. Don't say it with such excitement. It's not a hero's job.

JEREMIAH.   But you work there and earn money and . . .

ABEL.   Sack groceries. But it's a job.

JEREMIAH.   It sure is.

ABEL.   I don't know for how long, though.

JEREMIAH.   What do you mean?

ABEL.   There's a lot changing, and I mean . . . it's hard to have the last name of
             Montgomery around here without getting a lot of grief from a lot of
             people.

JEREMIAH.   Why?

ABEL.   My father doesn't exactly have a sterling reputation for being a friend of
             the community.

JEREMIAH.   But that's what his calling is. He's supposed to anger people, to make
             them cringe in the waste of humanity that they are.

ABEL.   There you go. See. That's the problem.

JEREMIAH.   What?

ABEL.   You can't have his view of people and get along with them. You can't
             hate them and think they are excrement and have them embrace you and
             want you to work for them and with them.

JEREMIAH.   That's the evil way of the world, though.

ABEL.   No. That's the hateful way of my father. There's a difference. And that's
             why there's going to be a major change soon.

JEREMIAH.   What do you mean?

ABEL.   Why did you want me to meet you out here?

JEREMIAH.   I wanted to talk.

ABEL.   Yeah, but why here? We're two full miles outside Damascus.

JEREMIAH.   I thought that we . . . I mean . . . I like it here, and . . .

ABEL.   And that we could fish? (*walking toward Jeremiah*)

JEREMIAH.   Yeah.

ABEL.   Or walk?

JEREMIAH.   Yeah.

ABEL.   Or swim?

JEREMIAH.   Maybe.

ABEL.   What is in that mind of yours, Jeremiah?

JEREMIAH.   What change?

ABEL.   What?

JEREMIAH.   You just said there's going to be a major change. What change?

ABEL.   I have to do something big.

JEREMIAH.   Big?

ABEL.   I can't live like this much longer.

There is an awkward silence. Then Jeremiah hugs Abel tightly. Abel doesn't know how to respond, but then lightly hugs him back.

JEREMIAH.   (*During the hug*) It'll be okay. Don't worry. Things will be okay. People are just bad, but we have each other. We are the elect. We're part of the family. You are the son of a great man. And I love you.

ABEL.   Jeremiah.

JEREMIAH.   I do. I love you. I love you.

ABEL.   Jeremiah. Thank you. (*breaks the hug*) I think the world of you, too. But I don't think I'm the son of a great man.

JEREMIAH.   Of course, you do! Your father is RC . . .

ABEL.   . . . Montgomery. I know. I've lived with that all my life.

JEREMIAH. He's . . .

ABEL.   . . . a tyrant.

JEREMIAH. Abel!

ABEL.   It's true, Jeremiah. You just don't see it. You can't see it.

JEREMIAH. Abel.

ABEL.   I have to . . .

JEREMIAH. (*Putting his hand on Abel's shoulder and rubbing it and his upper arm.*) You are so much like him. You have that force of character, that roar in your voice.

ABEL.   (*Moving away*) Jeremiah, you're so young.

JEREMIAH. Young? I'm a man now. I'm sixteen years old. I'm a man in every way, physically, mentally, AND spiritually. And I'm just a little younger than you. You're just nineteen.

ABEL.   Nineteen years here in Damascus, under . . .

JEREMIAH. You have so much going for you.

ABEL.   I'm leaving.

JEREMIAH. What do you mean?

ABEL.   I'm leaving Damascus.

JEREMIAH. You mean you're going to another town to work?

ABEL.   No, I mean that I'm leaving this place for good.

JEREMIAH. What?
ABEL.   I've joined the army, and I'm going to see the world. I'm going to try to take in as much of this planet as I can and see what's so bad about it that makes my father hate it so.

JEREMIAH. The army?

59

ABEL.   Yes, the army.

JEREMIAH.   But the army does the dirty work of this vulgar nation.

ABEL.   Jeremiah.

JEREMIAH.   You can't join the army. You'll never fit in. That's not you.

ABEL.   It's exactly me. I need this. I have to leave this pit of hatred and constant screaming and find who I am.

JEREMIAH.   You know who you are. You're Abel Montgomery. And you're right near perfect in every way. You look good. You act good. You are . . . good. And you're the son of RC Montgomery, the man who has looked after me and taught me and . . .

ABEL.   Jeremiah.

He hugs Jeremiah. Jeremiah holds him tight. After about five seconds, Jeremiah violently breaks the hug.

JEREMIAH.   No! Get your hands off of me, you pervert!

ABEL.   What?

JEREMIAH.   I know what you are! And you're touching me all . . .

ABEL.   Jeremiah! What are you talking about?

JEREMIAH.   I know what you're up to! You're a pervert! You're trying to touch me.

ABEL.   I am not!

JEREMIAH.   Joining the army! Out to see the world. I see what's going on. You're out to try every kind of rebellion and sedition you can to fight against your father. It's not going to work with me.

ABEL.   Jeremiah Coffee!

JEREMIAH.   Don't you use my name, you filthy pervert. The army, huh? It figures. The army. Wait until I tell your father.

ABEL.   I haven't got the chance to . . .

JEREMIAH.   I'll tell him. And I'm going to tell him what kind of a pervert he has for a
             son. That's why you were wanting to go swimming with me!

ABEL.   You're the one who asked me to . . .

JEREMIAH.   It all makes sense now! You got me to think highly of you. I'm glad that
             God opened my eyes! You're hell-bound. Go to your army. Go to your
             perversion. The whole world will burn with you and for you. You might
             as well leave now. When your father finds out about you, he'll disown
             you. I know him. I know him a lot better than you. You're nothing like
             him. Leave. Just leave.

Jeremiah runs off, back to Damascus.

SCENE 25: WHAT WE WANT TO SEE

BARLOW.   This is Mandy Barlow.

BRADFORD.   Ms. Barlow, this is James Bradford, pastor of the . . .

BARLOW.   Oh, I know who you are Reverend Bradford. We just aired a show
             about your . . .

BRADFORD.   Oh, I know what you just aired your show over.

BARLOW.   Is there something wrong, Mr. Bradford? We did our best to show what
             those vile people were doing to your church when they protested against
             you and the family of Nathan Pennington.

BRADFORD.   You showed that they're vile.

BARLOW.   And they are.

BRADFORD.   Yes, ma'am. But the way you framed the argument, Ms. Barlow, the lady
             you brought to debate Isabel Coffee didn't try merely to refute those
             horrible protests but to destroy faith itself, even what we stand for at our
             core.

BARLOW.   It's my job to bring the American people what they want to see.

BRADFORD.   That's not what the American people want to see.

BARLOW.   That's not what the polls indicate.

BRADFORD.   Where? In your ivory tower circles? That's not America.

BARLOW.   It's becoming America, Mr. Bradford. Day by day.

BRADFORD.   Show by show?

BARLOW.   I'm just exposing the underbelly of life, Mr. Bradford. I'm all about truth.

BRADFORD.   Truth? Somehow, it's being diluted into God knows what.

BARLOW.   Surely, He does, sir. Have a good day.

SCENE 26: THE SPOTLIGHT

BARLOW.   Ladies and gentlemen, welcome again to American Spotlight, where we
             talk about things of importance in our country. Remember, you are in my
             light. Well, they are up to it again. The so-called members of the Elect
             Street Church from Denver made their way to Richmond, Virginia to
             Saints Way Christian Fellowship, home of the Rev. Dr. James Bradford.
             Once again, they were protesting a funeral, once again the funeral of a
             fallen American serviceman, Marine Sergeant Nathan Dothan Pennington.

*Upstage, we see several protesters holding picket signs with anti-American (or BLANK)
      propaganda.*

BARLOW.   As the funeral honoring the memory of Pennington was occurring, several
             church members were spewing their brand of Christian hate speech
             outside the ceremony and at passersby.   Tonight, we discuss these events.
             Tonight, in our No-Holds-Barred Shoot Out Segment, we have the one
             and only Isabel Coffee, daughter of Pastor Jeremiah Coffee, hate monger
             and humanity hater, live from our affiliate in Denver.

Isabel Coffee enters DR and stands DR, facing straight ahead.

BARLOW.   Thank you, Ms. Coffee, for joining us.

ISABEL.   Thank you, Ms. Barlow.   Hate monger is a harsh moniker, but it's your
             show.

BARLOW.   Indeed, it is. And joining Ms. Coffee in the Shoot Out is president of the
             American Atheists Unity Coalition, Ms. Andrea McRae Lanier.

Andrea Lanier enters DL and stands DL, facing straight ahead.

BARLOW.   Good evening, Ms. Lanier.

ANDREA.   Good to see you again, Mandy.

BARLOW.   Let's get loaded and get started. (*Pause.*) Ms. Coffee, why does your church protest at the funerals of various Americans, causing them further undue grief?

ISABEL.   It's our job to point out that America and indeed the world is going straight to hell, almost everyone, and that dead soldiers, among others, is one of God's ways of letting you know that you're on a path of destruction.

BARLOW.   Ms. Lanier, does that sound unreasonable to you?

ANDREA.   Unreasonable, yes. Unexpected, no. It's basic Christian teaching that the world is doomed. These people are just honest enough to show the hatred that religion brings.

BARLOW.   But, surely you don't associate the actions of the Elect Street Church with all religions?

ANDREA.   Of course, I do. They are a Christian group. They represent the whole.

BARLOW.   Ms. Coffee, do you represent the whole?

ISABEL.   We most certainly do not. We are doing what we are called to do. The rest of so-called Christianity is weak in its ways and just like Ms. Lanier, godless, seared, and hopeless.

BARLOW.   Ms. Lanier, are you embracing the rest of religion that Ms. Coffee is sending your way?

ANDREA.   Never, Mandy. Don't let her fool you. She is just one of them. All faith is foolish and leads to dangerous results.

BARLOW.   Ms. Coffee, you lead a pretty dangerous group, don't you?

ISABEL.   Dangerous how? For speaking our minds? For practicing our First Amendment rights to say what we know to be true the same way that Ms. Lanier here is using her rights to speak her thoughts?

ANDREA.   But there is a difference. Mine doesn't hurt others.

ISABEL.   Neither does mine.

ANDREA.   It hurts feelings.

ISABEL.   So what? Where is it against the law to hurt feelings? Free speech is free speech or it's not free.

ANDREA.   Perhaps it shouldn't be.

BARLOW.   All right, ladies.

ISABEL.   Did you hear what she just said?

BARLOW.   I said, "All right, ladies." Ms. Coffee, you have law degree from Yale, is that right?

ISABEL.   Yes, I do.

BARLOW.   That is rather surprising.

ISABEL.   Why is that surprising?

BARLOW.   Because someone who is so educated usually isn't . . .

ISABEL.   A person of faith?

ANDREA.   Yes!

BARLOW.   So intolerant of others.

ISABEL.   Where is it stated that I have to be tolerant of others?

BARLOW.   Well, in your holy book, you are asked to . . .

ISABEL.   Where?

BARLOW.   Well, the Golden Rule is about . . .

ISABEL.   It's not about tolerance, and it's not about everyone.

BARLOW.   But putting others' feelings first is surely a tenant of Christianity.

ISABEL.   In some versions, I suppose.

ANDREA. See, Mandy. There you have it. We're not talking about a lack of education or a willing ignorance. Religion itself, faith itself brings close-mindedness and has its converts paint everyone else with its own brush. The whole lot of them is just alike, all of them hate and spew hatred. Faith is blight upon the planet, and this woman represents every one of them because secretly they are all just like her. I am disgusted.

ISABEL. Did you hear what she just did? Making me . . .

BARLOW. Enough, Ms. Coffee. We are tired of you and yours and what all of you promote.

ANDREA. She could have waltzed right into Bradford's church, and he and his kind would have welcomed her with open arms. There is no difference.

ISABEL. Wait a minute!

BARLOW. I told you, Ms. Coffee. We've heard enough from you. There you have the Shoot Out for tonight, America. We'll be back with the B Block in four minutes. Keep the lights on.

SCENE 27: A, B AND NO C

A teacher enters holding two large signs: one with a large letter "a" on it, with a "no crossbar" across it and one with a large letter "b" with rays of sunshine around it.

TEACHER. Today's Algebra lesson. If A is not true, therefore B must be true. Right? If A is repulsive and disturbing, any and all alternatives must be accepted. Isn't that logic? But wait, don't equations have C in them sometimes, too? Or is it too much for us to ask people to contemplate a C option? Or is it just easier for us to hate hatred and nothing more? But aren't we all about what's easy? That's Algebra. Right?

SCENE 28: LEND ME YOUR EARS

DMITRI. *(talking to someone offstage)* Oh yeah? That's not possible. I couldn't do that with a stick, especially not sideways. *(to Betty)* What are people thinking? You Americans are so detailed with your instructions.

BETTY.   Don't worry about it, Dmitri. You just have to be careful who you make mad. You really rub people the wrong way sometimes.

DMITRI.   What? No. No. I do not massage people any more. I gave that up two years ago when I started getting better roles.

BETTY.   Not literally, Dmitri. Not real rubbing. Irritating people. Bothering them. Getting in the way? Frustrating them?

DMITRI.   That's quite a list.

BETTY.   Just defining it for you.

DMITRI.   I guess I just need to stop talking then.

BETTY.   Like that would be possible.

DMITRI.   You'll see.

CALEB enters, dressed as Mark Anthony.

CALEB.   Betty! Dmitri! (*He hugs Betty, shakes Dmitri's hand.*)

BETTY.   There's my handsome Mark Anthony. So manly and masculine.

CALEB.   Wait 'til you see Portia.

DMITRI makes a groaning noise as if he wants to talk.

CALEB.   I'm telling you, Dmitri. She could pass for Brutus. And I'm talking about the one in Popeye.

DMITRI makes another noise as if he wants to talk.

CALEB.   What's wrong? What's wrong with him?

BETTY.   I think that he's trying to prove that he can refrain from talking.

CALEB.   Dmitri? Refrain from talking? Are we placing bets on how long it'll last?

DMITRI makes yet more noise as if he wants to talk.

BETTY.   How long until curtain?

CALEB.   We have about forty minutes I think. I'll have to get back in the dressing room in a few minutes.

BETTY.   So, we made it just in time to see you, then? (*She holds on to him.*)

CALEB hugs her back, puts his face close to hers.

CALEB. Yes, you did. You're always just in time.

NATHAN walks up.

NATHAN.   Caleb?

CALEB.   Nathan!

NATHAN.   I hope it's okay. You said I should just tell them that . . .

CALEB.   No! It's great. Nathan, this is Betty, fellow Broadway actress and my, well my, uh, are we using the, uh, word . . .?

BETTY.   Yes, whatever word you want.

CALEB.   This is my girlfriend.

BETTY.   Nice to meet you, Nathan.

NATHAN.   The pleasure is mine.

CALEB.   And this is my friend and also an actor here on the Great White Way. Dmitri.

NATHAN.   Nice to meet you, Dmitri.

DMITRI.   Thank you. Nice to meet you, too. Totally.

CALEB.   Why didn't I bet actual money?

NATHAN.   What?

DMITRI.   Forget it.

CALEB.   Guys, this is my friend, my very good friend, Nathan Pennington.

SCENE 29: WAITING ROOMS

Hospital waiting room. The sounds of elevator music are obvious, then subtly fade. Lisa and James Pennington are there. James is pacing in the waiting room, and Lisa is sitting, talking on her cell phone.

LISA.   Yes, Mary Ann. Yes, this is Lisa.

JAMES.   (*to himself*) I can't believe this.

LISA.   I just wanted you to know that Rachel is in labor. Yes, I know. They just came out and said that it won't be long at all now.

JAMES.   Totally uncalled for.

LISA.   Hold on, Mary Ann. (*to James*) Calm down, James. This is the way the world works. That's how babies are born.

JAMES.   Not with my baby giving birth, though.

LISA.   She'll be fine. Everything will be fine.

JAMES.   It had better be.

LISA.   (*back on phone*) James is really nervous.

JAMES.   I'm not nervous.

LISA.   He says he's not nervous, but he is.

JAMES.   I am not.

LISA.   And for an attorney, he's a rotten liar.

JAMES.   She's my little girl.

LISA.   (*to James*) Who's about to have her own little boy.

JAMES.   I know.

LISA.   Your grandson.

JAMES.   I know.

The doctor enters.

DOCTOR.   Grandma, grandpa?

LISA.   (*to the phone*) Gotta go.

DOCTOR.   I have someone I'd like for you to meet.

RACHEL's husband, TREY enters in medical gear as well, holding a baby.

JAMES.   I already know him. That's my son-in-law.

LISA.   (*hitting his arm*) Oh, James. Hush.

TREY.   Mom, Dad, please meet Blake Dothan Grierson.

They quickly go to the child and admire him.

LISA.   Awwww! Sweetheart! My baby!

JAMES.   Hey, little man!

LISA.   Look at him, James. He has Rachel's nose.

JAMES.   Yes, he does.

LISA.   And Trey, he has your mouth.

Lt. Col. Alex Marshall and another marine enter the waiting room.

MARSHALL.   Mr. and Mrs. Pennington, I hate to bother you here. I've been looking for you everywhere. You are not an easy family to track down.

JAMES.   May we help you?

MARSHALL.   I'm afraid that I have some bad news for you.

LISA.   Nathan?

MARSHALL.   Yes, ma'am. Concerning your son, Sergeant Nathan Pennington.

LISA begins to collapse. James catches her.

SCENE 30: 'TIS BUT A VAPOR

Steam room. A man sits, leaning back, eyes closed. Caleb and Nathan enter wearing towels. Caleb hobbles.

CALEB.   I can barely walk.

NATHAN.   You're doing fine.

CALEB.   No. I'm dying here.

NATHAN.   You'll live, cowboy. You kept up well.

CALEB.   I don't ever think I've worked out like that in my life.

NATHAN.   You're a New York actor. You keep in shape.

CALEB.   Not like a Marine!

NATHAN.   It's just a little more intense.

CALEB.   A little? I feel like I've given birth to a Jeep.

NATHAN.   That's why we're in the steam room. It'll help a lot.

CALEB.   Help? It's an absolute necessity!

MAN IN TOWEL. What's up?

CALEB.   Sup?

NATHAN.   Sup?

CALEB.   It hurts to breathe.

NATHAN.   It'll pass. Where'd Dmitri go?

CALEB.   I don't know. I guess we lost him. Probably talking to some random person about some random thing. I don't random know. I'm dying.

NATHAN.   Quit being a baby. I'm proud of him.

CALEB.   Who?

NATHAN.   Dmitri. He was with me every second and never seemed to break a sweat. He could be special ops.

CALEB.   What was up with that? Of all people I figured couldn't survive military death training, I never would have thought Dmitri.

NATHAN.   He's Russian.

CALEB.   What does that mean?

NATHAN.   I don't know. They're resilient.

CALEB.   Okay. Right now, I don't care.

NATHAN.   You'll be okay.

CALEB.   Sometime next month.

NATHAN.   You're crazy.

CALEB.   I've been told that.

MAN IN TOWEL. My first wife was crazy.

NATHAN.   Sorry to hear that, man.

CALEB.   Yeah. Sorry to hear that.

MAN IN TOWEL. No problem.

NATHAN.   So, Caleb. When did you get in from Denver?

CALEB.   Night before last. Late. I had meetings with my new director yesterday at 2. Translated: I haven't slept.

NATHAN.   See. That makes your workout even more impressive.

CALEB.   Did anyone ever tell you that you're an encourager?

NATHAN.   Once or twice.

MAN IN TOWEL. My third wife was an encourager.

NATHAN.   Really?

MAN IN TOWEL. Yeah. Always happy.   She was a counselor.

CALEB.   Ah.

MAN IN TOWEL. Absolute Frosty the Snowman all the stinkin' time.

NATHAN.   I guess she waved goodbye saying, "Don't you cry. I'll be back again someday."

MAN IN TOWEL. That's pretty much impossible. Unless zombies actually exist. She's pretty much dead.

NATHAN.   I'm sorry.

MAN IN TOWEL. I'm not. She wasn't my favorite person.

CALEB.   Okay.

MAN IN TOWEL. Spontaneous combustion.

CALEB.   Spontaneous combustion?

MAN IN TOWEL.   I know. I know. People say it's a myth, but I watched it go down. That happy camper was so full of internal hidden evil that she just went up in smoke one day. I saw it with my own two eyes. It was wicked cool.

Silence.

MAN IN TOWEL. Well, all this talk of fire and ice has me wanting a cigarette. I've pretty much been baked like a turkey in here. I'll leave it to you ladies. *Ciao.*

He exits.

NATHAN.   So.

CALEB.   Yeah.

NATHAN.   Anyway. Your rehearsals starting up for the new show this week?

CALEB.   No. Well, officially they are, but I won't be there.

NATHAN.   Why not?

CALEB.   I'm opting for a smaller role in this one. That's one of the things I needed to talk with the director about.

NATHAN.   Is something wrong?

CALEB.   Not "wrong." I just have to go back to Denver again next week for a little
           while.

NATHAN.   Again? Why?

CALEB.   Long story.

NATHAN.   We're in a steam room. I'm sweating. This place is melting off the bad
           things. I have time.

CALEB.   Nathan, there are so many things you don't know, that almost nobody
           knows. And they wouldn't make much sense.

NATHAN.   Try me. Unless you don't want me to know. And if so, I respect that.

CALEB.   No, it's not that. It's not you. *(Pauses)* Ugh. Why don't I just run my
           little law office outside the city, have my receptionist, take care of easy
           cases, make money?

NATHAN.   You have an office just like that, remember?

CALEB.   I know. I mean why can't I just do that and be content with that life:
           building a reputation, hiring a few partners?

NATHAN.   Yeah? Why *can't* you do that? I'll be out of law school soon!

CALEB.   I guess I wasn't born to that fate.

NATHAN.   What's that supposed to mean?

CALEB.   Sometimes we're born into different realities.

NATHAN.   You're not making a whole lot of sense, Caleb.

CALEB.   I know. Vagueness as a defense.

NATHAN.   You should know me by now. You don't need a defense with me.

CALEB.   I know. Ugh.

NATHAN.   This isn't the Caleb Martinez I know. The man I know is all courage and
           brass.

CALEB.   The man you know is Caleb Martinez, Yale lawyer and Broadway actor.

NATHAN.   And that's not you?

CALEB.   Yeah. That's me all right.   But you know that old saying about all of us
            wearing masks?

NATHAN.   Sort of.

CALEB.   Some of us don't wear them. They're in our genetics.

NATHAN.   I don't follow.

CALEB.   My blood, Nathan. Who we are beyond what we do.

NATHAN.   Okay. You're Caleb Martinez. Is there something about the Martinez
            family that I haven't heard about? Martinez? Hmn. Some famous mass
            murderer?

CALEB.   It's not the Martinez side.

NATHAN.   Okay. Who was your mom's family then?

CALEB.   Is.

NATHAN.   Okay. Well, who IS your mom's family then?

CALEB.   My mom is Isabel Coffee.

NATHAN.   Isabel Coffee. Coffee. Doesn't ring a bell.   The only Coffee family I
            know of are those religious nutjobs that hate America and protest at all
            those funerals.

CALEB.   Yeah.

NATHAN.   So, other than that, I can't think of any other Coffees.

CALEB.   You don't have to.

NATHAN.   Huh?

CALEB.   Those are the ones.

NATHAN.   What?

CALEB.   Those are the ones.

NATHAN.   Are you kidding me?

CALEB.   I wish I were.

NATHAN.   Your mom is related to those people who are on TV all the time arguing with everyone?

CALEB.   No, my mom IS the one on TV all the time arguing with everyone.

NATHAN.   That's your mom?

CALEB.   Isabel Coffee. Mouthpiece of the Elect Street Church in Denver, Colorado and spokesperson for the Coffee family.

NATHAN.   So, your grandfather is . . .

CALEB.   Jeremiah Coffee himself.

NATHAN.   Man.

CALEB.   To put it mildly.

NATHAN.   I would never in a million years had . . .

CALEB.   Good and thank you. Don't get me wrong. I love my family. I really do. I mean: they're my family. That's my mom.

NATHAN.   (*in shock*) That's your mom . . .

CALEB.   Dear ol' mom.

NATHAN.   What happened to you?

CALEB.   I don't know. I mean: I love them and all, but I've sort of gone my own path.

NATHAN.   You think?

CALEB.   There are some similarities. My mom and my grandfather both have law degrees from Yale.

NATHAN.   Oh, man.

CALEB.   Yeah.

NATHAN.   They attended Yale Law?

CALEB.   And graduated with honors. They're no fools.

NATHAN.   Wow. This is just crazy.

CALEB.   Yeah.

NATHAN.   And you've kept all this in?

CALEB.   Kept it in? Well, it's who I am. I generally choose not to discuss it.

NATHAN.   Wait a minute. They're Yale Law School graduates . . .

CALEB.   . . . with honors.

NATHAN.   . . . with honors—and they spew all that hatred?

CALEB.   Yep.

NATHAN.   They believe all that garbage?

CALEB.   Every word. They think that everything is in moral downfall and that America's to blame.

NATHAN.   Wow. Well, the downfall may be right.

CALEB.   Yeah. I do think they're right on that, but they go too far.

NATHAN.   Yeah. A little.

CALEB.   Yeah.

NATHAN.   Wow.

CALEB.   So, now you know my big secret.

NATHAN.   That's pretty big.

CALEB.   It is.

NATHAN.   Hey. Don't worry about it. My uncle's a Jehovah's Witness.

CALEB.   Nathan.

NATHAN.   Okay. Okay. No comparison. I know. (*Pause*) How did Betty take it?

CALEB.   She doesn't know.

NATHAN.   Seriously?

CALEB.   It's not something easy to bring up.

NATHAN.   Dmitri?

CALEB.   Nope.

NATHAN.   Okay.

CALEB.   No one except you. And Dr. Barker.

NATHAN.   Dr. Barker?

CALEB.   Yeah. She figured it out.

NATHAN.   How could she "figure it out?"

CALEB.   It's a long story. And that's why I've been going to Denver recently. It's really her idea.

NATHAN.   I'm so very confused.

CALEB.   To be honest, I am, too.   Listen, I may be going somewhere else, too, and I really need some advice.

NATHAN.   From me?

CALEB.   We all have our areas of expertise, and I need to tap into yours.

NATHAN.   I'm at your service.   Where are you going?

CALEB.   We may be taking the new show on tour.

NATHAN.   Nice. Where?

CALEB.   The Middle East.

NATHAN.   The Middle East?!

CALEB.   Yeah. The playwright's from Israel, and the director's actually originally from Jordan. They're wanting to take it back and perform it in both countries for authenticity or something. The want the actors oriented to the culture.

NATHAN.   Wow. The Middle East.

DMITRI enters wearing a towel, too. He is talking to someone outside the door.

DMITRI.   Okay. Okay. I'll say it just once. Gee! "Captain, Captain. I 've locked phasers on the Klingon vessel." Are you happy? I don't know what these people want. Hello, Caleb. Hello, Nathan.

CALEB.   Dmitri.

NATHAN.   Hey, Dmitri. 'd you get lost?

DMITRI.   No. I've just been talking with some people in the showers. I like this place.

NATHAN.   Good job with the work out today. You really kept up.

DMITRI.   Children's play. I tell you. The children's play. When you grow up in Russia and travel the world, you learn to tough out the life.

CALEB.   You sure outdid me.

DMITRI.   Oh, Caleb. You haven't had to fight to live like I did. You have had it easy. Lap of luxury. Caring family. I have traversed deserts, climbed mountains, swam oceans. Just to live. That's why I act now. I can use my body for beautiful things now. I even walked through Jordan once. I heard you mention it when I walked in.

CALEB.   You've been to Jordan?

DMITRI.   Twice.

Caleb looks at Nathan.

DMITRI.   What?

CALEB.   Nothing.

DMITRI.   I am a man of the world. By the way, Jordan sucks. It's ugly. And hot.

CALEB.   We need to talk about your experiences, Dmitri. I may need some of your insight.

DMITRI. Sure. I will tell you all I know. And when you go to Russia, I can tell you so much that you will be at home even before you arrive. I know it like the back of my arm. In fact, I am a walking map for Russia.

NATHAN. You know a lot about the countryside?

DMITRI. Yes. But I also mean that I am a literal walking map of Russia. My body corresponds to the motherland. See. (*Points to random places on his chest, neck, and arms*) This is Moscow. This is Balashikha. And this (*lifts right arm and even uses his arm as part of the map*) is the Khimki Forest, just northeast of Moscow proper. It is a beautiful forest, makes me homesick. Oh, and this is Domodedovo Moscow Airport. I am telling you. These are exact proportional dimensions. I have measured and checked them to scale. (*Hits his diaphragm*) This is Kotelniki. And this is highway M4.

Nathan and Caleb stand and leave.

DMITRI. What? Why you leave? I am just getting started. I am literally a map of all of Russia. You will know it before you get there. Wait. I haven't got to the Kremlin! Or Siberia!

SCENE 31: VIDEO #178

Documentary-like music underlies this entire scene. ACTOR 2 walks by with a sign that reads "GODHATESYOUSOVERYMUCH.COM."

JEREMIAH. Welcome. This is video number 178 on our web series of eternal realities. God sends pain and disaster. You heard me, and you know. Think of the horrible things that have happened to this nation. Over and over again, this country goes into shock over the disasters that come flying at their family and friends. When are you going to wake up? Are you perverted AND stupid? God sends the crises! Those slices of hell are straight from God right at you. This nation embraces vile and sick deeds and has turned its back on God Almighty. Perversion. Fake preachers. All your talk of grace and love. There is no grace. You have no love. God hates you. He hates you so much that He sends death to wake you up. But it is to no avail. There is no waking you up. It's too late. You have paved your path to hell. There is no hope. If God even could hear your prayers, I would say just pray that sudden death hits you before you face fire from Heaven. There is no hope. There is no grace. Stay tuned for video 179. And have a nice day.

SCENE 32: THE SHADOW OF GREATNESS

TOWNSPERSON 1. Why are you here?

PROTESTER 1. Because we have a right to speak our minds!

TOWNSPERSON 2. Why are you doing this?

PROTESTOR 2. To show America why it's going to hell.

TOWNSPERSON 1. You're at a funeral of a brave and beautiful American soldier who laid down his life for your freedom.

PROTESTOR 1. That's why it's called freedom! And more and more soldiers will die. God kills them, your sons and daughters will die because of this sick, perverted country.

TOWNSPERSON 2. You're here at one of the biggest theological seminaries in the country, a place that teaches the Bible for Heaven's sake! Why would do this?

PROTESTER 2. This is a vile excuse for a school, teaching false doctrine, not even half-truths, more like three-percent truths! This is the heart of the problem. This is where the evil begins. This is where the "pervert" nation gets its nutrition!

TOWNSPERSON 1. You dare say that God kills American soldiers.

PROTESTER 1. I do.

TOWNSPERSON 2. You dare say that God hates America.

PROTESTER 2. God hates you. God hates your prayers.

Isabel sits, editing at the computer. Caleb enters.

CALEB. So, Mom. You're into web development now?

ISABEL. Caleb. You're here. When did you get back?

CALEB. This afternoon. I found a direct flight from New York.

ISABEL. Sin City.

CALEB.   I thought that was Vegas.

ISABEL.   They're all sin cities.

CALEB.   Mom, there are good and bad people everywhere.

ISABEL.   Caleb, what happened to you? I didn't raise you to be so accepting of so
           much wrong. This country is sick and disgusting.

CALEB.   (*Remains silent.*) So, you didn't answer my question. Are you working on
           the website these days, too?

ISABEL.   I've learned a lot the past few years that you've been away. I'm updating
           our protest dates and uploading a few new videos from some of your
           grandfather's sermons.

CALEB.   Granddaddy's sermons.

ISABEL.   Don't start. I don't want to hear it. You never understood that you grew
           up in the shadow of greatness.

CALEB.   Okay.

ISABEL.   What? No sarcastic remark? No witty comeback? No Broadway retort?

CALEB.   No. Not anymore.

ISABEL.   Wait. Why? I know you too well. You're not waking up? What's on your
           mind?

CALEB.   I want to talk.

ISABEL.   About?

CALEB.   I want to know what happened to my dad.

ISABEL.   Caleb, we've talked about this as much as . . .

CALEB.   No. We haven't. We've talked about it as much as you care to talk, but
           that's not enough. I'm sorry if it's hard on you or difficult to think about,
           but I have to know.

ISABEL.   Caleb, you ask too much.

CALEB.   Isabel Coffee Martinez, what happened to my father?

SCENE 33: EYE ON COFFEE

ELI.   Good evening, I'm Eli Connor, and you're watching Eye on the World, where we look where we're not supposed to look so you can know the truth around you. There's a lot going on the planet tonight, so we need to get started. Today's opening statement: What makes a zealot tick? We're live in Denver, Colorado, and we're here with an exclusive interview with America's most hated minister, the Reverend Jeremiah Coffee. Coffee is the leader of the controversial Elect Street Church here in Denver. He and his group gain publicity almost weekly for their protests of military funerals, churches, seminaries, public events, museums, and the like. With their well-known picket signs decrying God's hatred of America, American soldiers, Jews, gays, preachers, politicians, and just about anyone else, they constantly rile up America's anger. Add that to appearances on talk shows, and they are America's most hated family. This is the interview that American has been talking about, and it is here.

SCENE 34: ALLEGIANCE

STUDENT.   (*holding the American flag*) I pledge allegiance to the flag of the United States of America and to the republic for which it stands, one nation, under God, with liberty and justice for all.

SCENE 35: FACES OF STONE

An actor walks by with a large poster of Mount Rushmore.
Outdoor, random location near Mount Rushmore.

Jeremiah Coffee is standing, looking around.
Two Secret Service agents approach.

AGENT 1.   Mr. Coffee.

JEREMIAH.   Yes.

AGENT.   Sir, the Senator will be arriving soon. We'll need to pat you down and
            check your person if you don't mind.

JEREMIAH.   Of course. (*He puts his arms in the air.*)

AGENT 2 pats down and checks COFFEE. The agent finds two items.

AGENT 2.   Sir. Just a cell phone and a small book.

JEREMIAH.   That small book's the Bible.

AGENT 1.   You can keep your Bible, but I'll need to hold on to your phone until the
            meeting is over.

JEREMIAH.   If you must.

AGENT 1.   (*Talking into a radio on his arm*) He's clear. All's clear. Agent Monroe
            and Donovan are on the perimeter. Everything's good. You can send the
            Senator in.

*SENATOR ALAN MICHAELS enters. He is confident, but it's obvious he is
uncomfortable.*

MICHAELS.   Thank you, gentlemen. I can handle this from here.

AGENT 1.   We'll be right over here, sir.

MICHAEL.   Thank you.

The AGENTS step offstage.

JEREMIAH.   Good afternoon, Senator.

MICHAELS.   Mr. Coffee, why am I here?

JEREMIAH.   I guess that's a question you'll have to ask yourself.

MICHAELS.   Let's cut the BS, Coffee. When I got your request to meet, the first thing
            I did was laugh, but for some reason, I have been asked by some very
            persuasive people to go ahead with this meeting.

JEREMIAH.   That it would be in your best interest?

MICHAELS.   Those were the exact words. Yes. Mr. Coffee, please allow me to be
            totally and painfully direct. I don't like you. I have never liked you. I
            find you, what you say, what you do, what you orchestrate, how you judge

and hate, everything about you to be disgusting. It makes me want to vomit.

JEREMIAH. Okay.

MICHAELS. And yet here I am. I am meeting with someone whom I define myself as the opposite of in every way. I stand for everything you're against. And for the record, I don't share any single one of your beliefs. I think they're primitive, backward, and Neanderthal.

JEREMIAH. Senator Michaels, I can assure you that I'm not recording our meeting. I know you're running for President, but there's no digital device here. I promise. There's no need to go on the record so strong.

MICHAELS. Coffee, I'm just speaking my mind.

JEREMIAH. Well, I can't blame a man for that.

MICHAELS. Why am I here?

JEREMIAH. I think we can help each other out.

MICHAELS. Help each other out? Why would I . . .

JEREMIAH. Hear me out.

MICHAELS. You brought me all the way to South Dakota to . . .

JEREMIAH. You were already in Iowa campaigning.

MICHAELS. But this is not Iowa. Mr. Coffee, I'm afraid that this is a waste of time.

JEREMIAH. You want to be President of this nation?

MICHAELS. Pardon me?

JEREMIAH. You heard me. I asked if you want to be President of this nation.

MICHAELS. Well, I *have* officially declared my candidacy, so yes, I think it's pretty obvious.

JEREMIAH. You could use my help.

MICHAELS. Are you kidding?

JEREMIAH. Not in the slightest.

MICHAELS. If anyone even found out that I was having a passing conversation with Jeremiah Coffee, my career would be over.

JEREMIAH. No one will ever find out.

MICHAELS. I can *assure* you that I don't need *your* help for my run for President. In fact, I'm the very last person that you'd ever vote for. I stand for everything that you're against. I can't think of one reason why you would ever consider supporting me or one reason why I would ever take any assistance from someone that epitomizes everything I despise.

JEREMIAH. Let's cut all the insults and head to the heart of the matter, Alan.

MICHAELS. What?

JEREMIAH. You've been a US Senator for over fourteen years. You're not stupid. You know the way things are done. You've bought into the machine in Washington, the vile and filthy cesspool of the sin factory, putting out the disgusting, pathetic laws that go all against all things good.

MICHAELS. Wait a minute.

JEREMIAH. You're not stupid. In fact, you're pretty savvy. You know how to get things done. And you know how alliances are made. What I don't understand is how you don't know how someone gets to be President.

MICHAELS. I'll have you know that I've run three very successful campaigns in which my people and I . . .

JEREMIAH. Three campaigns where you traveled your entire state in a car in one day, talking to people who think like you and look like you. There are millions and millions of people out here who are not like you in the slightest.

MICHAELS. And they're certainly not like you.

JEREMIAH. Oh, I know that. And I am grateful. For me.

MICHAELS. You just need . . .

JEREMIAH. Would you shut up and listen to me for a minute. Get your head out of your ego and shut up a minute.

MICHAELS. Ego?? You're . . .

JEREMIAH. I can make sure you're President.

MICHAELS. You?

JEREMIAH. Yes. You have no idea the resources I have, the funds available to be used how I decide. Volumes that would have your big city donors look like gravel.

MICHAELS. A person is only allowed to donate . . .

JEREMIAH. Allowed? Allowed? When are you going to start thinking like a President. Certain words should not be in your vocabulary.

MICHAELS. You have to hate me. You hate what I stand for. I am for all the things you label as sinful and worldly. I call them freedoms. You doom people to hell.

JEREMIAH. I do. Guilty on all counts. I don't have to agree with you to help you.

MICHAELS. You want me to be President when I will do everything in my power to promote everything that you hate?

JEREMIAH. Coalitions are made for reasons, Alan. Throughout history, strange bedfellows have changed history. There's not a President in US history that didn't get there without the explicit help of his enemies. Undergrad minor at Yale.

MICHAELS. *You* attended Yale?

JEREMIAH. Why is that so hard for everyone to believe?

MICHAELS. Tell me why.

JEREMIAH. Why what?

MICHAELS. Why do you want me to be President?

JEREMIAH. You need it spelled out then?

MICHAELS. Please. I'm a Senator. Put it in small words.

JEREMIAH. You and I disagree on every fundamental and moral and religious issue possible.

MICHAELS. Yes.

JEREMIAH. You are the perfect example of everything that is wrong with our modern society.

MICHAELS. Thank you.

JEREMIAH. But unlike every other candidate, and unlike any other candidate we've ever had, you go farther.

MICHAELS. Go on.

JEREMIAH. You want to go deeper and deeper in debt. That doesn't bother you.

MICHAELS. Now, that's a matter of . . .

JEREMIAH. Let me talk. I'm not criticizing you on it. I'm agreeing.

MICHAELS. Go on.

JEREMIAH. You want to introduce so many regulations on any and everything that American business may not be able to survive one term of your Presidency. You despise our military, and you want to demobilize them. You think America has been a force for evil on the planet and that we should back off and allow other countries to lead on world issues. You'd support any and every social issue that I honestly believe would bring the nation down so quickly that it will turn on itself with bloodshed. You would be the most controversial and damaging President in history. As a result, I want to help you succeed. I, too, for totally different reasons think this nation is a horrible place as is. And I have total faith in your ability to help bring about its destruction. I want to help you.

MICHAELS. (*Stunned, walking, thinking*) Your reasons are insulting and idiotic. I should expose you to the nation as . . .

JEREMIAH. Senator.

MICHAELS. I know. If I were to accept funds and other resources from you . . .

JEREMIAH. No one would ever know. Ever.

MICHAELS. And you would expect that . . .

JEREMIAH. I would expect from you that you do exactly as you want to do it. And fully expect my public criticism.

MICHAELS. And you're serious about this?

JEREMIAH. Senator, there is a reason your advisors told you that you should meet with me. I can help you in ways that you could never imagine. I am not some backwoods hillbilly, some TV preacher begging for money. I have funds that I can put at your disposal that will make you the most formidable candidate the US has seen in decades. And it'll all look perfect, every "t" crossed and "i" dotted. I give you my word.

MICHAELS. Coffee, you better not be yanking my chain.

JEREMIAH. Talk with your advisors.

MICHAELS. (*Silence*) How do we . . .

JEREMIAH. I'll contact your guy in about week. I can get most of it started by then.

MICHAELS. You're not what I expected.

JEREMIAH. Well, if you don't mind my saying, you're exactly what I expected.

AGENT 1. (*Entering*) Sir, it's best that we be going now. There's a crowd of tourists coming in on buses.

MICHAELS. Right. Thank you.

JEREMIAH. Senator, it was a pleasure to meet you. (*offers his hand, Michaels does not shake it*) Senator, do we have a deal? Will you accept my help?

MICHAELS. Talk to my people next week.

JEREMIAH. I will.

MICHAELS. (*Starts to leave*) We do not know each other. In any way.

JEREMIAH. In any way.

MICHAELS. Okay. We have a deal.

JEREMIAH. Good.

MICHAELS. And I hate everything you stand for.

JEREMIAH. And I hope you rot in hell—eventually.

MICHAELS nods to the AGENT who gives JEREMIAH back his phone.
MICHAELS and the AGENT leave.
JEREMIAH smiles.

SCENE 36: MY KINGDOM FOR A HORSE

Dmitri is sitting in his dressing room, taking off his makeup. There is a knock at his door. When he answers the door, Caleb and Betty enter.

DMITRI.   Betty! Caleb! You're here. I was scared that you hadn't made it.

BETTY.   We were here, silly boy. We just got here too late to come see you before the show.

DMITRI.   But you did see it?

CALEB.   Of course!

DMITRI.   And . . . ?

CALEB.   I loved it.

DMITRI.   Really?

CALEB.   Really. It was good. "Now is the winter of our discontent
           Made glorious summer by this sun of York."
           I mean: who would have thought that you'd have pulled off the hunchback Richard III so well?

BETTY.   They made a great casting choice. You actually played Richard.

DMITRI.   Thank you?

BETTY.   You know what I mean.

DMITRI.   I'm telling you. You get a role in a Lee Lawson show, doors open everywhere.

CALEB.   Not that again.

DMITRI.   One show. Association. Doors.

BETTY.   Dmitri.

DMITRI.   Doors.

BETTY.   I know.

89

CALEB.   Nevertheless, good show. Nice concept.

DMITRI.   Even the human stairs.

CALEB.   That got kind of old.

BETTY.   Hurry up, silly boy. Caleb and I are taking you to dinner.

DMITRI.   What?

CALEB.   Yeah. Our treat. We can't let an opening night bang end with a whimper.

JEREMIAH   (*entering, dressed to the nines*). Ah, T.S. Eliot. "This is the way the world ends, this is the way the world ends, this is the way the world ends. Not with a bang, but a whimper."

DMITRI. May I help you?

JEREMIAH.   I don't know about help, per se. I was hoping for an invitation to dinner, though.

DMITRI.   What? I'm flattered and all, but . . .

BETTY.   You're Jeremiah Coffee.

JEREMIAH.   You have a keen eye.

BETTY.   THE Jeremiah Coffee.

JEREMIAH.   I don't think there's another.

DMITRI.   Who's Jeremiah Coffee?

BETTY.   What are you doing here?

DMITRI.   Who's Jeremiah Coffee?

BETTY.   One of the most reprehensible human beings on the planet.

JEREMIAH.   Well. I see we're off to a good start.

CALEB.   Betty.

DMITRI.   What are you talking about?

BETTY.   Jeremiah Coffee, the preacher of that church from Denver that goes
            around protesting at all the funerals with their hateful signs and bashing
            everyone and everything from gays to Jews.

DMITRI.   Oh?

BETTY.   Spewing hatred and disdain.

CALEB.   Betty.

DMITRI.   What are you doing here?

BETTY.   Yeah. What ARE you doing here? This seems a little out of your league.
            I figured you'd be crawling under some log somewhere.

JEREMIAH.   You see, people assume that when you disagree with them, that they must
            be some sort of uneducated, backwoods buffoon. I warned you about that
            before you headed to the big city, Caleb.

BETTY.   Wait. Caleb? What? You know this man?

DMITRI.   He warned you?

JEREMIAH.   Is this young lady a close friend of yours, Caleb?

BETTY.   Caleb? *(confused)*

DMITRI.   Oh, they're more than friends. I mean, I am a friend, but not like that.

BETTY.   Caleb?

JEREMIAH.   *(to Dmitri)* I did come to see your production tonight, young man. I've
            always had an affinity for Shakespeare, nearly everything he wrote, as
            sinful and vile as he was. The Duke of Glouster truly holds a special place
            in my heart.

CALEB.   Betty. This is my grandfather.

BETTY.   What?

DMITRI.   Thank you. This is one of the favorite roles I have ever taken up.

BETTY.   Your grandfather?!

CALEB.   Yes.

BETTY.   You're a Coffee?

JEREMIAH.   Just half. He has other blood flowing through his veins, too.

DMITRI.   I'm so glad you came.

BETTY.   Dmitri!

DMITRI.   What?

BETTY.   (*to Caleb*) I can't believe this.

CALEB.   Betty.

BETTY.   I need some air. (*She storms out.*)

JEREMIAH.   You might want to go check on your lady friend.   Then you and I need to
have a little man to man.

Caleb follows Betty out.

DMITRI.   So! You're a fan of the theatre?

JEREMIAH.   No. Not at all. I can't stand it. I don't like your queer creations.

DMITRI.   (*Confused*) What?

JEREMIAH.   I said that I don't like your godless smut.

DMITRI.   But you just . . .

JEREMIAH.   Don't get too close. I said what I needed to say.

DMITIRI.   You mean you didn't come see . . . I mean, Shakespeare.

JEREMIAH.   No.

DMITRI.   I don't understand.

JEREMIAH.   You're Russian.

SCENE 37: SLINGS AND ARROWS

Outside the funeral of Nathan Pennington.

PROTESTER 1.   You are going to burn in hell.

PROTESTER 2.   THE USA DESERVES DAMNATION.

PROTESTER 1.   Thank God for dead soldiers!

PROTESTER 2.   Thank God for killing Nathan Pennington.

CITIZEN 1.   What did you say?

PROTESTER 2.   Thank God that he took out Nathan Pennington.

CITIZEN 2.   Look! You can't say that.

PROTESTER 2.   We can say what we want. Freedom of speech.

PROTESTER 1.   It's our job to speak the truth.

CITIZEN 1.   The "truth"? Why are you saying these things?

CITIZEN 2.   Are you trying to convert people to your ways?

PROTESTER 1.   There's no conversion for you.

PROTESTER 2.   There's no hope for you.

PROTESTER 1.   You're a nation of filthy perverts.

CITIZEN 1.   But you're slandering an American hero, and a man who just laid
                 down his life for his friend. It doesn't get more noble than that.

PROTESTER 1.   Man's nobility is worthless rags. God killed the soldier.

CITIZEN 1.   Just stop. That's enough. You can spew your poison all you want,
                 but quit saying that about Pennington.

PROTESTER 2.   We won't stop.

PROTESTER 1.   We will speak our minds.

PROTESTER 2.   You're damned, and your flesh will rot forever.

PROTESTER 1.	God hates you. God hates America.
PROTESTER 2.	God hates the American soldier.
PROTESTER 1.	God kills the soldier.
PROTESTER 2.	Thank God for killing Nathan Pennington.
CITIZEN 1.	That's it! I'm gonna kick your . . . !

A full-fledged fistfight breaks out. After the seventh or eighth blow, that fight goes into slow motion and highly emotional operatic music plays—as the next scene begins.

As the next scene goes on, the fight goes on and slowly moves off-stage.

SCENE 38: THE PIROUETTE

Another fistfight moves onto the stage from SL. It's obvious that the fight is being fought with teen students from several decades ago. The fighters are a sixteen-year-old Jeremiah and another teenaged boy. Three students rush on as onlookers.

TEENAGER 1.	Let him have it, Frank!
TEENAGER 2.	Show him what's up, Frankie!
TEENAGER 1.	Make him eat dirt!
TEENAGER 3.	Come on! Teach him a lesson.

Jeremiah is definitely losing this fight.

FRANK.	You like this, Coffee? You enjoying this, you traitor? Traitor!
JEREMIAH.	Quit calling me a traitor!
FRANK.	Well, what else are you? Turning on your country. Badmouthing!
JEREMIAH.	I'm speaking the truth.
TEENAGER 2.	You ain't speaking no truth. You're crazy.

JEREMIAH.   I'm standing up for what's right.

Frank hits him again—hard.

FRANK.   Does that feel "right?"

TEENAGER 1.   Woo-eee! Look at that blood!

TEENAGER 3.   How does that feel, Coffee?

JEREMIAH.   May God damn your souls to hell!

FRANK.   There you go again.

Frank kicks him.

JEREMIAH.   Damn you , damn you, damn you!

FRANK.   Quit your trash talking!

JEREMIAH.   The whole country! And your soldiers! A bunch of liars and
                    cowards just like you!

The beating continues until Lydia runs in.

LYDIA.   Stop! What do you think you are doing!?

They stop, step back and watch her go to him.

LYDIA.   What are you doing? Are you all right?

FRANK.   (*to Jeremiah*) Think about it!

LYDIA.   Get out of here.

FRANK.   Don't forget this, Coffee.

They leave, laughing.

JEREMIAH.   Don't worry. I won't. Ever.

LYDIA.   Are you okay?

JEREMIAH.   (*getting up, wiping blood off with the back of his hand*) Yeah. I'm
                    okay. Let me stand up. Hold on.

LYDIA.   Let me help you.

JEREMIAH.   No. Leave me alone.

LYDIA.   What?

JEREMIAH.   Leave me alone. Let me get up myself.

LYDIA.   What's going on?

JEREMIAH.   Nothing.

LYDIA.   It's not nothing. That boy didn't beat you up for nothing.

JEREMIAH.   He didn't beat me up.

LYDIA.   He was hitting you.

JEREMIAH.   We were fighting.

LYDIA.   You know better than that.   We don't believe in fighting.

JEREMIAH.   You don't believe in fighting.

LYDIA.   You don't believe in fighting, either.

JEREMIAH.   Yes, Momma. I do. I do believe in fighting. There are some
                things that have to be fought over.

LYDIA.   What's happened to you? What's happened to my son?

JEREMIAH.   Nothing.

LYDIA.   No. Something has happened to you. You've changed. You've
                been acting different for over two months now. You came home
                one evening quiet and angry. You stopped talking to me. You've
                been gritting your teeth and pouting and just angry at the world.

JEREMIAH.   The world is an evil place. It's godless and demonic and
                worthless.

LYDIA.   Jeremiah, the whole world isn't evil. There are good people.

JEREMIAH.   No! There aren't. People are wicked. They're hateful. They're
                liars and tricksters and perverts. And they are out there
                everywhere, even filling the army with their vile perversion, out

	there taking arms to defend a nation full of sinners and deceivers and men who lie with men. No one. There's no one to trust. And I won't. It's me and mine. God has let me know. Me and mine. God hates everyone else, EVERYONE else. They're all going to hell, and they have no hope.
LYDIA.	Jeremiah.
JEREMIAH.	No. All of them. Hell. God hates America. God hates them. He hates them for what they are and what they have become. It's too late.
LYDIA.	But, Jeremiah . . .
JEREMIAH.	No, Momma. No. I know my calling. You're my momma, and your part of the protection of God, but all these people are going to face the wrath of God. They can plead and beg with Him all their lives. He doesn't love them. He doesn't love them. Even the ones who think they are His chosen. Even preachers and their families. None of them. It's over. He hates them.
LYDIA.	Oh, son.
JEREMIAH.	I want to go home.
LYDIA.	Son.
JEREMIAH.	Yes?
LYDIA.	(*Pauses*) Let's get you home and cleaned up.

They exit.

SCENE 39: THE TIES THAT BIND

ACTOR 1 walks by holding a sign that says "VACANCY."

DONNA MARTINEZ, a woman in her mid 70's works the front desk at a motel. CALEB enters.

DONNA.	Good afternoon. Welcome to The Eagle Talon Inn. May I help you?

CALEB.   Well, I hope so.

DONNA.   Do you need a room for this evening? We have a few vacancies left.

CALEB.   I was hoping to talk with you about something else.

DONNA.   Oh. Okay. What can I help you with?

CALEB.   I need to speak with Donna Martinez.

DONNA.   I'm Donna Martinez. Do I know you?

CALEB.   I certainly hope so.

DONNA.   Oh. For the record, I don't owe you or any company you represent a penny. I have paid off all of my debts finally, and I don't need anybody coming to harass me about anything.

CALEB.   Well, my intent isn't to harass. I promise you.

DONNA.   It'd better not be. I've been through enough in my life that I can tell you that I can take care of my myself.

CALEB.   That's good to hear.

DONNA.   Who are you then?

CALEB.   Well, that's the thing. My name is Caleb, Caleb Martinez.

DONNA.   (*Pause*) Martinez. Caleb. (*Recognition*) Caleb. Oh.

CALEB.   Yes.

DONNA.   Oh! My dear Caleb.

CALEB.   Grandmother?

DONNA.   Oh, yes. (*Grabbing him and hugging him*) Grandmother. That's perfectly fine. Oh, my boy. Oh, my boy! I never expected . . .

CALEB.   I know.

DONNA.   How did you ever find me?

CALEB.   That's a long story.

DONNA.   Whatever are you doing here?

CALEB.   That's a longer story.

DONNA.   How did you make it through all the layers of your life to get here?

CALEB.   That's the longest story of all.

DONNA.   A story that I can probably tell for you. I have a feeling that I know it well.

CALEB.   Yes, you're Donna Martinez.

DONNA.   Oh, my dear sweet boy. I haven't seen you since you were tiny. So tiny. And you're not any more. You're such a man.

CALEB.   Thank you.

DONNA.   So much like your father. So much like my boy, my sweet boy.

CALEB.   Grandmother?

DONNA.   Yes, darling?

CALEB.   I need to know. That's part of the reason I'm here. I need to know.

DONNA.   Oh, Caleb. What can I say? What can I tell you? It's been so long.

CALEB.   I need the truth. All I get is half truths and dodges. I can't bear it any more.

DONNA.   I know, sweetheart. I know.

CALEB.   What happened to you? What did they do to you? What happened to my father? Please tell me.

DONNA.   Your father was a good boy. He was so kind and so sharp and so genuine. He didn't deserve all the things he went through.

CALEB.   What happened?

DONNA.   I don't know what to say. I guess I'm to blame for how things happened. I don't know.

CALEB.   Don't say that. I know the circumstances you were under must have been stressful. Remember: I grew up in Denver.

DONNA. It's not that simple. And it didn't start in Denver.

CALEB. Okay. I know they moved there before I was born.

DONNA. Yes, they, well, we did.

CALEB. Please tell me what happened exactly.

DONNA. Caleb, how did you find me?

CALEB. I have my ways. I'm pretty resourceful. I have friends all over New York, Connecticut, and the East Coast.

DONNA. Please tell me that you didn't go to Yale.

CALEB. Yale Law School. Why?

DONNA. (*laughs*) It's in the blood, isn't it?

CALEB. I guess it's an involuntary tradition. But without that, I wouldn't have found you.

DONNA. It was Claudia, wasn't it?

CALEB. Yes.

DONNA. Dr. Claudia Barker. She lives to set wrongs right.

CALEB. That's what we're supposed to do, isn't it?

DONNA. Yeah, but sometimes the guilty get hurt with the innocent.

CALEB. Don't you mean the innocent get hurt, too?

DONNA. No. That always happens anyway. I mean the guilty get what's coming to them even though they try to avoid it.

CALEB. Tell me what happened. There's so much that has to be addressed, so much I need to know. There comes a point where things have to be dealt with. The story has to come out and be told. Justice has to be served.

DONNA. Spoken like a young, idealistic lawyer.

CALEB. Not so idealistic. Just wanting to get to the truth and see how this all needs to play out.

DONNA.   A dramatic lawyer. Gracious, it's a good thing you didn't attempt acting.

CALEB.   Well, actually . . .

DONNA.   Community theatre? Heavens, I'll bet Jeremiah passed out.

CALEB.   Well, I actually have my law practice on a little bit of a hold. I work a few shows on Broadway.

DONNA.   (*Laughs*). Good Lord! It's amazing he didn't have a heart attack! Hell fire and damnation on the whole lot of you!

CALEB.   I'm family, remember?

DONNA.   Right.

CALEB.   What happened to you, Grandmother? Please. You can tell me. And what happened to my dad? Please.

DONNA.   (*Pause*) It was Damascus, Kansas. A long time ago. I was Donna Sue McDaniel, I was young, and I married Joseph Martinez, the cousin of Jeremiah Coffee. Of course, that was before he became the Jeremiah Coffee everybody knows today. And not the one I would know.

SCENE 40: SURPRISE!

ISABEL.   I can't believe it. I cannot believe it.

DAVID.   (*following, dressed in a military uniform*) What?

ISABEL.   I can't believe you went and did it!

DAVID.   What do you mean?

ISABEL.   You joined the army? The army, David?

DAVID.   Would you rather I'd joined the navy?

ISABEL.   You can drop the sarcasm.

DAVID.   What do you expect me to say?

ISABEL.   I don't expect anything now.   You've already said everything.

DAVID.   Isabel, I told you I wanted to do this. I've told you this from day one.

ISABEL.   And I told you from day one that you couldn't do it.

DAVID.   That I couldn't do it? Not permitted? Is that what you're saying?

ISABEL.   David, what am I going to tell Dad?

DAVID.   I don't care what you tell him.

ISABEL.   Yes, you do. David, you do!

DAVID.   Isabel . . .

ISABEL.   You know what our stance on the military is. You know the army is the evil arm of this Satanic country.

DAVID.   Isabel . . .

ISABEL.   This is a sick and disgusting place that God hates to the core, and you just put yourself into the heart of the beast.

DAVID.   It's the right thing to do.

ISABEL.   The right thing to do? Do you know what I put on hold for you? We've been married less than a year. Less than a year. I can tell you this: I'm going back to law school now.

DAVID.   If that's what you think you want to do.

ISABEL.   Oh, I will. I will.

DAVID.   Okay.

ISABEL.   But I'm going to wait a few months before I do.

DAVID.   Isabel, I'm going to be deployed, and we . . .

ISABEL.   I'm going back to Yale. But after the baby.

DAVID.   If you want to . . . (*Pauses, shocked*) what?

ISABEL.   That got your attention, didn't it? Yes. I'm pregnant. Surprise.

SCENE 41: THE ENVELOPE

DAVID.   Mom.

DONNA.   What is it, David?

DAVID.   I, um, . . .

DONNA.   What is it, David? Why did you want to meet me here? Is there something wrong with Isabel?

DAVID.   I, uh, need your help.

DONNA.   How?

DAVID.   I'm in trouble, and I don't know how it happened.

DONNA.   What?

DAVID.   There was a, uh, an envelope on the door this morning. And it was addressed to me.

DONNA.   Yes.

DAVID.   Mom, I am so sorry. I don't know what happened.

DONNA.   Tell me.

DAVID.   You know how excited I am about joining the army. I have wanted to do it for so long, and I know it's not what you wanted. I know it's not in line with what you believe with, you know.

DONNA.   What is this about?

DAVID.   This envelope had a letter in it and some photographs.

DONNA.   What kind of photographs?

DAVID.   They were photographs of, photographs of me, in some . . .

DONNA.   In what?

DAVID.   In some very bad situations.

DONNA.   What do you mean?

DAVID.   In some very provocative, personal situations with someone.

DONNA.   David. You mean . . .?

DAVID.   They were bad. Very bad.

DONNA.   With a woman other than Isabel?

DAVID.   With someone else.

DONNA.   You were with another woman?

DAVID.   No, Mom. Not exactly.

DONNA.   Oh, David. No.

DAVID.   No, Mom! I didn't do it. I never would have done anything like that.
            That's not me. I mean I married Isabel because I love her and . . .

DONNA.   Oh, David.

DAVID.   Mom, listen to me! I did not do those things in the photos. I did not.
            Something's bad wrong. And the letter is a threat. It's threatening
            specially to tell Isabel and even Jeremiah if I . . .

DONNA.   If what?

DAVID.   Whoever it is wants me to meet them on the roof of the Cranford building
            in downtown Damascus tomorrow night at midnight.

DONNA.   Meet them? Why? What do they want?

DAVID.   Oh, mom. They want $30,000 cash.

DONNA. $30,000?

DAVID.   By tomorrow night. Or . . .

DONNA.   We don't have that kind of money. We should go to the police.

DAVID.   Mom, those photos are so real-looking. I've never seen anything like it.

DONNA.   David, you swear to me that you didn't do those things!

DAVID.   Mom, if I did, I was drugged or something. You know I was sick a few
            days ago and couldn't keep anything down. I thought it was the flu, but
            now I don't know.

DONNA.   So those photos . . .

DAVID.   Could have been staged.

DONNA.   Oh, David. Who was the other person in the photo?

DAVID.   I don't know! I have no idea.

DONNA.   Oh.

DAVID.   Mom, you've got to help me.

DONNA.   I don't have that kind of money.

DAVID.   But Jeremiah does.

DONNA.   David.

DAVID.   He has it in cash.

DONNA.   David.

DAVID.   He has so much that he'd never miss it. You've told me that hundreds of
            times.

DONNA.   David.

DAVID.   You're there every day. You're practically his treasurer.

DONNA.   David, that's theft.

DAVID.   Mom, I'm being blackmailed. And it's pretty real. The photos are real.
            Imagine what would happen if Jeremiah found out. Just imagine.

DONNA.   Oh.

DAVID.   And there's something else I have to tell you.

DONNA.   I don't know if I can handle anything else.

DAVID.   Isabel's pregnant.

DONNA.   Pregnant? That's wonderful. (*Beat*) Oh. Oh.

DAVID.   Mom, you have to help me. You have to.

DONNA.   Oh.

SCENE 42: ROOFTOPS

*On the roof of the Cranford Building, midnight. We hear the church tower strike twelve.
During the strikes, David enters.*

DAVID.   Hello? Anybody here?

A dark figure approaches.

DAVID.   Hello.

FIGURE.   Did you bring the money?

DAVID.   Yes.

FIGURE.   All of it?

DAVID.   Yes.

FIGURE.   Where'd you get it?

DAVID.   It doesn't matter. Here. Come and take it. It's yours.

FIGURE.   Yes, it is.

DAVID.   You have to destroy all evidence of those photos. That's the deal. Isabel
            and Jeremiah cannot see them.

FIGURE.   We have to figure out the deal. I just told you to meet here and bring the
            money.

DAVID.   What a minute. I recognize your voice.

FIGURE.   You do?

DAVID.   Jeremiah?!

JEREMIAH.   You're not as dumb as you look.

DAVID.   What's that supposed to mean? Jeremiah, why are you . . . ? What's
            happening here?

JEREMIAH.   Well, on one level, I'm here to get my money back.

DAVID.   Back?

JEREMIAH.   Yes, back. Just knowing that it's been out of the safe for six hours is
            enough to make me antsy.

DAVID.   You knew?

JEREMIAH.   That Donna stole it from me?   Oh, yeah. That was the plan. I knew that
            you'd have to have her to do that.

DAVID.   What?

JEREMIAH.   There was surely no other outlet for you to come up with $30,000. I knew
            that if I put that amount in the letter, you'd have to contact your mother,
            and then as easy as that, she would commit a crime, a crime I have on
            video now.

DAVID.   You wrote the letter?

JEREMIAH.   Indeed. And sent you those rather explicit photos.

DAVID.   Why would you send me a letter asking for money that was going to be
            yours? And why would you even . . . ? I'm confused.

JEREMIAH.   David. David. I got my money back. And now, I have something to use—
            proof of your dear mother stealing from me. Let's call it leverage.

DAVID.   For what? Why?

JEREMIAH.   To fix a few problems.   Now, as for those photos . . .

DAVID.   I don't understand those. I never, NEVER did that in my life. I don't
            know what happened, and I don't know who that person was with me.

JEREMIAH.   Just someone I hired.

DAVID.   What? You hired?

JEREMIAH.   That was you by the way. And you are rather difficult to move around
            while you're out.

DAVID.   God in Heaven!

JEREMIAH.   He's not available right now. We have business to attend to.

DAVID.   Jeremiah, you drugged me, staged vile photos of me in horribly
            compromising positions, blackmailed me, and had me make my mother a
            thief for money that was coming right back to you?

JEREMIAH.   There you go adding things up. I guess Isabel was right when she said you
            caught on to things eventually.

DAVID.   Why? Why are you doing this? What did I ever do to you?

JEREMIAH.   Isabel tells me that you joined the army.

DAVID.   Is THAT it? You hate the military so much that you would do all this
            because you're angry over my enlisting?

JEREMIAH.   Oh, no. It DOES disgust me and make me sick to my stomach that you
            would join such a collection of mercenaries doing the bidding of the
            perverts in Washington, but that's not it, and you know it.

DAVID.   What is it then?

JEREMIAH.   I need them back.

DAVID.   You need what back?

JEREMIAH.   Don't play dumb. I know you have them. You're the only person who
            ever goes into my study. You know you took them.

DAVID.   Jeremiah, I don't know what you're talking about.

JEREMIAH.   I'm not going to play this game. I have video of your mother stealing
            $30,000 from me. And I have photos of you in very vivid positions. I
            want my letters back, and I want you to go far, far away from here and
            never come back again.

DAVID.   Letters? Away from here?

JEREMIAH. I want them. I don't know if you've read them, but I suspect you have, and you are not welcome anywhere around here again. Anywhere. If you so much as think about contacting anyone from here, I will turn your mom over for theft and send your photos to the media.

DAVID. What? What are you talking about? Letters to whom?

JEREMIAH. The letters I wrote to someone named Abel. He was the son of my mentor and pastor when I was young. The letters were personal and private and were never sent. I should have never kept them, but I did. And you took them.

DAVID. Letters? Love letters to a man? Jeremiah.

JEREMIAH. (*Walking toward him*) Where did you hide them?

DAVID. Jeremiah, I never took any letters. You wrote love letters to a man? It all makes sense now. Every bit of it.

JEREMIAH. Shut up! Give me the letters and get out of here.

DAVID. I don't have your damned letters, and furthermore, I am tired of your intimidation and threats. It all makes sense now. And you drugged me and took those photos. You're a sick man! A sick man. And everyone's going to know. I'm not scared of you.

JEREMIAH. I demand you return those letters.

DAVID. What part of "I don't have them" don't you understand? And it doesn't matter—because people are going to know anyway. Your days of extortion are over. You may never see your grandchild.

JEREMIAH. Grandchild?

DAVID. Oh, has Isabel not told you? She's pregnant. She and I are going to be parents of a little Martinez, free of the influence of the big bad Jeremiah Coffee.

JEREMIAH, in a fit of rage, shoves David off the side of the building. Then he walks to the edge to see if David is dead.

JEREMIAH. I think not.

SCENE 43: TWO FOR TEA

CLAUDIA BARKER is sitting in her living room, reading, drinking a cup of tea. There is a knock at the door. She goes to answer it. Standing there, distraught is DONNA MARTINEZ.

DONNA.   Claudia?

BARKER.   Donna. Are you okay? What's wrong? (*She leads her inside to the couch.*)

DONNA.   Oh, Claudia.

BARKER.   Here. Take a seat. Can I get you some tea?

DONNA.   No, thank you. Well, yes, but in a few minutes.

BARKER.   I'll get you some. Are you okay?

DONNA.   Yes. No. No, not at all. I had no one else to go to, nowhere else to turn.

CLAUDIA.   It's okay. It's okay. You're always welcome here.

DONNA.   And I've bothered you.

CLAUDIA.   Not in the slightest. Just studying for the Bar. I needed a break. Donna, you never get out of Damascus. What are you doing all the way here?

DONNA.   Claudia, I'm in trouble. And some horrible things have happened.

CLAUDIA.   Like what?

DONNA.   And there is no one else in life to turn to. I mean, since Joe died—and now when I need him more than ever.

CLAUDIA.   What about David?

DONNA.   (*Crying*) Oh, Claudia! He's dead.

CLAUDIA.   Oh!

DONNA.   He committed suicide. Jeremiah found the note. He jumped off the top of a three-story building in Damascus.

CLAUDIA.   Oh, Donna. I'm so sorry. Why did he do it?

DONNA.   I can't talk about it much. And on top of that, on top of that. Oh.

CLAUDIA.   (*hugging her*) Oh, Donna.

DONNA.   I did something bad, really bad, and I can never go back there.   Jeremiah
            could ruin me, so he told me to leave. He told me to leave, Claudia!

CLAUDIA.   Oh, sweetie. In a way, that's good!

DONNA.   Good? My life was there! My family, except for you.   Everything.
            Everyone. And my David. And so much more.

CLAUDIA.   You couldn't have done anything *that* bad.

DONNA.   I did. Enough that I can't go back. And Jeremiah is moving everyone and
            everything out of Damascus anyway.

CLAUDIA.   What?

DONNA.   He's picking up the entire ministry and family and moving them all to
            Denver.

CLAUDIA.   Colorado?

DONNA.   There'll be nothing left in Damascus.   Nothing. It's the place that took
            my son's life.

SCENE 44: THE WILDERNESS

BETTY is sitting in a coffee shop. CALEB enters.

CALEB.   Betty!

BETTY.   My Caleb!

They embrace and kiss.

CALEB.   I'm pretty much in shock. What are you doing in Denver?

BETTY.   Well, I had to come see you.

CALEB.   I'll be back in New York soon.

BETTY.   I know, but I had to just come out here and see what's up, what's going on.

CALEB.   What's going on?

BETTY.   And I've actually never been to Denver before. This is my first trip to Colorado. I usually just look out the plane window on the way to LA and say, "Hello, little Rocky Mountains."

CALEB.   Well, here you are, then. Welcome to the Rockies.

BETTY.   To the Rockies. You want a coffee?

CALEB.   No, thank you. I'm glad to see you and all, but why are you here?

BETTY.   Caleb, after finding out about your family and all, I was in complete shock. It doesn't make a bit of sense. And then with you coming out here so many times, I just wanted to see what's going on, you know?

CALEB.   I don't know. To see what's going on? What do you mean?

BETTY.   You know. You've been coming out here so much recently. Spending time with these . . . people.

CALEB.   My family?

BETTY.   Caleb. Not really. You're nothing like them.

CALEB.   My family.

BETTY.   Sure. But more like a distant echo is something that you are not.

CALEB.   What?

BETTY.   This is a bad influence on you. You're not like all these people. I would never fall in love with a bigot.

CALEB.   I'm not a bigot.

BETTY.   That's what I'm saying. You're not. You don't hold on to these crazy ideas.

CALEB.   No, not at all.

BETTY.   You don't agree with all these protests and hateful signs.

CALEB.   No. I despise it.

BETTY.   Exactly. You don't down people and hate on others who think differently from you.

CALEB.   No.

BETTY.   And you don't take to all this God nonsense.

CALEB.   What?

BETTY.   You're not all religious like these nutjobs.

CALEB.   Well, if you're assuming that I don't believe in God . . .

BETTY.   Right.

CALEB.   You're wrong.

BETTY.   What?

CALEB.   I believe in God.

BETTY.   Oh, Caleb. You can't.

CALEB.   I can't? Why can't I?

BETTY.   You're such an intelligent, handsome, talented man. You can't believe in all that stupid backwoods nonsense.

CALEB.   I guess I'm not all those things then because I do believe in God.

BETTY.   But not a God who did the whole creation thing? Please tell me you're not one of those. Caleb, you can't be.

CALEB.   The whole creation thing? You mean, do I believe God created the universe and our planet? Yes, I do.

BETTY.   Caleb! You're a graduate of Yale Law School!

CALEB.   And?

BETTY.   They were supposed to get all that out of you.

CALEB.   Well, I'm sorry, Betty, but it's still *in* me. That's my belief. Just respect it. I don't insist that you see things my way.

BETTY.   Caleb.

CALEB.   What?

BETTY.   Caleb.

CALEB.   What??

BETTY.   The Bible. All those stories. All that mumbo-jumbo craziness. You're a lawyer. You're an . . . artist for . . . .well, goodness sake! You can't.

CALEB.   I can't what? And why can't I? Does it make me less intelligent in your eyes if I have faith? I don't understand. I'm not allowed to believe in God?

BETTY.   It's so silly. We know better now.

CALEB.   We know better? Look, if you don't want to believe in this or in anything, that's your right.   Seriously. But don't try and make me feel like I have something wrong with me, that I'm not working on all my cylinders if I don't see the world that way you do.

BETTY.   It's not just the way "I" see it. It's all of intelligentsia. It's the whole educated world, baby. And you've been corrupted by a hate-filled bigot.

CALEB.   My grandfather is a bigot. Yes, I'll give you that. He is a horrible human being and a bad example for everyone who knows him, but what he is and what he does has no bearing upon my faith in God.

BETTY.   Caleb, you know people can't live this way. If people found out, you'd be laughed out of everything.

CALEB.   I don't think so.

BETTY.   I do.

CALEB.   Then I don't care.

BETTY.   Caleb.

CALEB.   Betty, we're a combination of our memories, our experiences, the people in our lives, and our beliefs. Without those things, we are not ourselves, no matter who does or doesn't like it. I really don't care.

BETTY.   Please don't tell me that you're into grace and redemption and talking with God.

He just stares at her.

BETTY.   Oh, Caleb. You have to stop. I'm going to have to get an intervention together for you.

CALEB.   Stop.

BETTY.   Come on. Let's get back to New York. We need to get you back to the city. Caleb.

CALEB.   Betty, stop.

BETTY.   Caleb, I love you, and I can't stand this.

CALEB.   And you want me to renounce who I am?

BETTY.   Just this silliness. Caleb, you're a brilliant man.

CALEB.   Except for this?

BETTY.   Grace, Caleb. Prayer? A God who hears you? Genesis? Caleb, please.

CALEB.   All of it, Betty. It's who I am just as much or more than anything or anyone else.

BETTY.   Well, I, um. There's no way I can even start to believe that any of this is happening. There's no way that you can just sit there and tell me that you believe all this garbage.

CALEB.   Betty, that's enough. It gets insulting after a while.

BETTY.   And you don't think I'm insulted?

CALEB.   How? Because I have beliefs? You can't allow for me to have beliefs?

BETTY.   Not something stupid, no. And not something that would make you choose Him over me. No.

CALEB.   It doesn't have to be a choice.

115

BETTY.   Oh, but it does.

CALEB.   Then it's made.

BETTY.   And what it is?

CALEB.   Good-bye, Betty.

BETTY.   Caleb, this is ridiculous. You're an intelligent man.

CALEB.   Good-bye.

He exits.

BETTY.   Caleb Martinez, get yourself back here this instant and tell me that all of this is a joke.

SCENE 45: FLATS

Jeremiah Coffee is walking along a lonely road. It's obvious that he is frustrated.

JEREMIAH.   (*looking up*) I know You think this is funny. I really do. Two flat tires in the middle of Timbuktu, in the middle of zero traffic, none at all. Not one, but two flat tires. And on top of that, no cell coverage. None whatsoever. You just want me to walk. That's okay. I'll walk. I'm just five miles outside of Damascus. I can walk. And don't think for a moment that I'm not suspect of the irony of it all: the road to Damascus. But that's all right. It's all right. I know what I know, and all will be well. I'm going to be late, but all will be well. I'm just walking. It's not like I'm someone who needs a Damascus road exper . . .

He is frozen, wide-eyed. His mouth goes slightly ajar.

JEREMIAH.   Oh, my. Oh, my. Of course. Yes. Yes.

He rapidly continues walking toward Damascus.

SCENE 46: A PASSAGE TO DENVER

Rev. Bradford walks to his car, briefcase in hand. James Pennington approaches.

JAMES.   Jacob.

BRADFORD. James Pennington! I haven't heard from you or Lisa in weeks. I've worried about you both.

JAMES.   Thank you.

BRADFORD. I've called and even stopped by your house.

JAMES.   I'm sorry. We've been away a while. We each took a hiatus from work and left for a while.

BRADFORD. I understand.

JAMES.   We spent a little time with Rachel and Trey and the baby. And then we went to the beach house in Maine.

BRADFORD. Okay.

JAMES.   I, um, needed a little time to try to put this all into some sort of perspective, not that that can be done.

BRADFORD. No.

JAMES.   It doesn't make any sense.

BRADFORD. Losing a child never does.

JAMES.   Not at all, but it's more than that, Jacob. We lost Nathan, and we'll never have him again. And those people, those idiots with their signs and their hatred, outside the funeral. The gall! Their words and their cruelty.

BRADFORD. James, you have to let that go. They're stupid, stupid people.

JAMES.   I can't let it go. Right there at the funeral, Jacob. The one and only funeral for my only son.

BRADFORD. I know.

JAMES.   Lisa hasn't spoken in weeks.   I mean, she says what she has to, but
              generally she just stares out the window, just staring. No tears. No
              anything. Just staring out the window in silence.

BRADFORD. James, I am so sorry.

JAMES.   I'm going to see him.

BRADFORD. Who?

JAMES.   Coffee. The leader of those people.

BRADFORD. Are you serious?

JAMES.   Extremely.

BRADFORD. James, I don't think that's a good idea.

JAMES.   Good idea or not, I'm going. They're in Denver. They're as easy to find
              as they are at finding everyone else.

BRADFORD. And what do you plan to accomplish with the visit? If he'll even see you.

JAMES.   Oh, he'll see me. One way or another, he will see me. And I don't know
              what I'll accomplish. I have a few questions I want answered, a few
              things I need to say.

BRADFORD. You're walking into something a little bigger than you realize.

JAMES.   And what have I got to lose? My life has been stolen from me as it is. I'm
              not scared. There comes a point at which logic can keep you from doing
              what you have to do. I'm not going to let that happen. I don't care if it
              makes sense or if it's a really bad idea, I'm going. At the very least, I
              want some of my dignity back.

BRADFORD. And you're here to tell me because . . . ?

JAMES.   Well, I wanted you to know.

BRADFORD. And?

JAMES.   That's pretty much it.

BRADFORD. (*a deep breath*) And I should go with you.

JAMES.   No.

BRADFORD. I don't know what you have planned, but you don't need to go alone.

JAMES.   I don't need anyone with me. I have to do this alone.

BRADFORD. You can't handle this alone, James.

JAMES.   I . . . I just need answers. I don't know where else to turn. I . . . I need to know why and . . . I need . . .

BRADFORD. You need rest, James. Let me take you home. Lisa needs you.

JAMES.   I just don't understand.

BRADFORD. I know. Neither do I.

SCENE 47: THE BURDEN OF DAMASCUS

CALEB and DMITRI enter, looking around.

CALEB.   Well, I guess this is it. It's been a long time since I've been here. I don't know if I would have recognized it.

DMITRI.   This is the town that your family came from?

CALEB.   I guess this would be the one.

DMITRI.   It's so tiny.

CALEB.   It didn't used to be. To hear my mom talk, there was a time when this place was filled with people, especially when my grandfather was young. I guess things change.

DMITRI.   Things must have changed a lot here.

CALEB.   I think a lot of it had to do with everybody picking up and moving to Denver. I know when they moved the location of the church, a lot of people went, but the rest of the town just almost disappeared.

DMITRI.   Reminds me of a town I know of in northwestern Russia, a place called Ivangorod.

CALEB.   Please no human map this time.

DMITRI.   Oh, it would be up here. (*He touches the top of his right shoulder.*) It was a booming place until it just shriveled down. All the people moved to Narva, just over in Estonia. Crazy.

CALEB.   Well, I don't know if I'd call Damascus "booming," but it at least had a lot more life to it.

DMITRI.   There is a reason for all things. I have learned that.

CALEB.   I appreciate your coming out here with me. I know you don't leave the city too often these days.

DMITRI.   I never have a need to. I guess I'm spoiled. I didn't mind coming. I always wondered what Kansas looked like anyway. All I knew was Dorothy and the tornado.

CALEB.   I don't know if Damascus is an accurate representation of the state.

DMITRI.   I still can't get over how you Americans name your towns after other cities in the world. Damascus. Every time I hear it, I think of the real Damascus.

CALEB.   This is a real Damascus, too.

DMITRI.   You know what I mean.

CALEB.   I need to start looking, talking with a few people. There has to be some clue here, some reason to explain what happened to my grandmother and to my dad. She said that whatever it was happened here, right here. Something was so bad, so devastating that it changed the course of her life and made the family relocate. All my life, there's been something, something that was below the surface, something there I couldn't see or touch or even feel sometimes, but something that was always present, always lingering, always unwelcome yet demanding to be known. I'm tired of it. I am sickened by it, and I don't even know what it is. Are you okay?

DMITRI.   Yeah. I'm just listening.

CALEB.   No joke or unrelated red herring?

DMITRI.   No, I don't eat red herring anymore.

CALEB.   No, a red herring is . . .

DMITRI.   I *know* what a red herring is: a tangent, an unrelated anecdote.

CALEB.   Yeah.

DMITRI.   Yeah.

CALEB.   Well, okay.

DMITRI.   Good! What do you want me to do? Do we need to pull some good-cop, bad-cop routine? I can be out-of-control if you need me to.

CALEB.   We just need to fish around. Ask questions about things that happened years ago. My dad's name was David Martinez. My grandmother was Donna. Just see who remembers what. She said that if wanted to know, I'd have to start here. I couldn't get much more out of her. Every time we started, she'd almost hyperventilate.

DMITRI.   I'll ask around. I'll look innocent. I'll play the uniformed foreigner, okay?

CALEB.   Okay! Sounds good.

DMITRI.   (*walking off SR).* Oh, hello, ma'am! Is that a knish? I would know for you see: I am from Mother Russia. And the rumors are true, all of them. Ma'am!

CALEB.   (*to himself, talking about something completely different)* The rumors are true? Ugh. I only wish I had a rumor to start with.

JEREMIAH.   (*walking up slowly from US)* Rumors are dangerous things. They can get you in a lot of trouble.

CALEB.   (*truly startled)* Grandfather! What . . . What are you doing here?

JEREMIAH.   I really should be asking you that question. This is a long way from a Manhattan loft.

CALEB.   And a long way from Denver.

JEREMIAH.   Not that far. A few hours' drive for the right reason.

CALEB.   Why'd you drive out here?

JEREMIAH.   To see what you're up to.

CALEB.   Me?

JEREMIAH.   Yes. To see why you came all the way out here yourself.

CALEB.   I . . . Wait. How did you know I was coming to Damascus?

JEREMIAH.   Caleb. You know me. You know I know just about everything. For all
            the enemies I have everywhere, I have just as many friends. People let
            me know about the things I need to keep up front.

CALEB.   You've got spies watching me?

JEREMIAH.   Absolutely not. I have associates, employees who look out for our
            interests, not mine—ours.

CALEB.   I don't understand.

JEREMIAH.   You don't need to, my boy. You just need to trust me. You've always
            had a hard time with that. It's this perverted world we live in, the
            depraved existence of alcohol and sex and parties you live in. Oh, I know.
            I know, Caleb. But we're in for better days. Everything is about to get
            better.

CALEB.   What are you talking about?

JEREMIAH.   Why did you come here? (*Silence.*) You flew out here and brought that
            stupid little Russian with you. You left your lady friend back in Babylon,
            not that she's your lady friend any more after your meeting in Denver.

CALEB.   How do you . . . ?

JEREMIAH.   Caleb, do you really not understand? There are those who pull the strings.
            Some do it openly. Some do it behind closed doors. And some do it
            seemingly openly but pull the marionettes behind the doors. Whoever's
            doing the pulling has to see the characters. You can't take care of things
            blindly. That's a lesson you'll have to learn as you step up to leadership.

CALEB.   You don't pull people's . . . Leadership?

JEREMIAH.   We'll get to that in a minute. Tell me about this fishing expedition you're
            on.

CALEB.   What?

JEREMIAH.   You and Little Stalin here. Why are you doing this? What are you trying to get at? It's pointless. It's a waste of time.

CALEB.   We're just trying to see . . . I want to know . . .

JEREMIAH.   This is all futile. There's nothing. There's no "here" here.

CALEB.   Then why did you come here to stop me?

JEREMIAH.   I'm not here to stop you. I'm here to save you a lot of time and a lot of pain. The past is a dangerous place, and the directions there have been changed by memory.

CALEB.   I need to know what's true.

JEREMIAH.   Good grief, boy! True? Life is filled with misery. That's true. Life is filled with godless people destroying the fabric of existence around us. That's true. Every form of perversion and power grabs surrounds us. That's truer than true.

CALEB.   That's not what I'm talking about. I'm talking about the truth.

JEREMIAH.   And what's true is that as a man you learn to deal with things and you learn to deal with not knowing things, and then you learn to take things that you wish you'd never known and put them somewhere where you won't and can't get to them any longer because if you knew where the key to the door was, you'd never let it go. You'd unlock the memories of things that you don't even know are true anymore or were possibly never true in the first place and revisit them. That's not being a man; that's being a child. "When I was a child, I spake as a child, I understood as a child, I thought as a child: but when I became a man, I put away childish things."

CALEB.   I want to know what happened here.

JEREMIAH.   I was on my way here a few hours ago, and I had two flat tires. Not one, but two. God has a way of talking to you and getting your attention. And I was thinking that here I was on my way to Damascus, coming to talk some sense into you, and then, walking on the road, I had a revelation. It's been years, but as sure as I'm standing here, I know what I heard.

CALEB.   This is insane. I need answers.

JEREMIAH.   You want answers? I'll give you answers! You want some truth heading your way? Open your ears, boy. God Almighty has some information for you. You are next.

123

CALEB.   What?

JEREMIAH.   You're next. You're to take my place.

CALEB.   No.

JEREMIAH.   Oh, yes. You're going to follow in my footsteps and carry on the work
            that must be done.

CALEB.   There's no way!

JEREMIAH.   And yet, it'll happen. God has ordained it and has spoken it. This world
            is dying, all its inhabitants on the path to the Lake of Fire, and you're
            going to be the beacon of truth to them all, telling them of God's hatred
            and disgust!

CALEB.   Why are you doing this?

JEREMIAH.   I'll continue to lead for the next eight years, at which time you'll step up
            and take my place as the new shepherd. Eight years will be enough time
            for you to straighten out your thinking.

CALEB.   What makes you think there's a slight possibility of that happening? You
            know that's not remotely possible.

JEREMIAH.   Time has a way of making the impossible quite probable.

CALEB.   No.

JEREMIAH.   Eight years is enough time for a man to make drastic changes.

CALEB.   What happened to my father?

JEREMIAH.   I have to start planning for the transition.

CALEB.   What happened to my father?

JEREMIAH.   I'll have to let your mother know how we're going to do this. There are
            money issues that you can't begin to fathom.

CALEB.   What did you do to my father? Did you kill him?

JEREMIAH.   Caleb. Would you listen to yourself! What's wrong with you?

CALEB.   I need to know what happened to him. What did you do to him?

JEREMIAH.   Caleb, your father was the victim of some major sin issues in his life, some demons in his character that unfortunately lead to his taking of his own life. The pathway of sin leads to destruction, both in body and in soul.

CALEB.   And how did you end up with his suicide letter?

JEREMIAH.   Your father trusted me completely. He battled with his sin nature and eventually succumbed to it, but he knew enough to let me know what he chose to do.

CALEB.   And his mother?

JEREMIAH.   His mother?

CALEB.   Donna. What did you do to her?

JEREMIAH.   Caleb, you have to be careful how you process information you've been given. You're a Yale graduate. You know better.

CALEB.   No. I used to. I don't know better anymore.

JEREMIAH.   There's wisdom in leaving well enough alone. That's maturity. Some answers you don't want. That's common sense.

CALEB.   That's why I'm here. Answers.

JEREMIAH.   No. It's not.

CALEB.   What?

JEREMIAH.   That's not why you're here.

CALEB.   Yes, it is.

JEREMIAH.   No, it's not. You're not here for answers. You're here for relief. You're here for catharsis. You have this burning and yearning in your soul, a thirst that can't be quenched. And you're trying your best to find answers to questions that don't even exist.

CALEB.   You're infuriating! I'm asking these questions! They exist!

JEREMIAH.   No, they're filaments of a reality you hope to be true because of your world sense of justice. I'm telling you something that you will find out soon: the only justice in the world is the justice of the Lord God Almighty and his soon-coming wrath upon everyone and everything not under His tent of protection. There is not justice with man. Man uses story and memory to change facts. There are facts, Caleb. There are facts, and they have been taunted and manipulated and destroyed by people who don't like the truth and who want to change existence to cover up who and what they are. Bad things have happened in this town, lots of bad things. There are events that occurred here that I don't want to remember, but they happened. But they won't happen again. I can promise you that.

CALEB.   What's that supposed to mean?

JEREMIAH.   Your father died here. It was an unfortunate event. If I had been there, I would have done everything in my power to stop him.

CALEB.   What do you mean—they won't happen again?

JEREMIAH.   This place, this town: it has too much. It has a demonic presence. It's a source of too many bad things, too many echoes.

CALEB.   You can't erase a whole town just because there are things here that you don't want thought about—or discovered.

JEREMIAH.   There are many things that you can do when you decide to do them.

CALEB.   You can't get rid of echoes by erasing the sound.

JEREMIAH.   But you can. Caleb, you can.

CALEB.   This is sicker than I thought.

JEREMIAH.   Damascus will become a heap of ruins and its power will end.

CALEB.   What do you intend to do? Kill people? Burn it down?

JEREMIAH.   Quit being so dramatic. There is way to solve problems without resorting to such extremes.

CALEB.   You're some sort of monster.

JEREMIAH.   And there goes the label. How many times have I heard that mantra: monster, villain, sociopath. It seems that's the verse sung by the world, those echoes of "tolerance" they scream about. This life is a war. Haven't you figured that out yet? A war. The culture war being raged over what direction this world is going. The political war with never-ending attacks over which "Nimrod" will be the next dictator. The social war on every media outlet and Internet outlet available. The international war about who hold whose land and uses whose resources and votes in whose election. And the spiritual war over who believes what and who should believe what about everything. And it's all in vain. It's a travesty. The whole lot of them are going around in circles like children on broken tricycles, spinning, playing with little minds, living in their depravity, feasting like there's no tomorrow, being Hedonists and epicureans and seeking their strange flesh and digging a pit in which they exist in squalor, with no hope of salvation, no hope of redemption, no hope of God's love ever, ever coming near to them, a mindless existence of blindness while God's hatred pours over them like rain. I'm not a monster. I'm nothing near a monster. I'm the only man on the planet who knows the total truth and the only one who can speak it. That's not a monster. That's a messenger.

CALEB. A town?

JEREMIAH. It will be taken care of. The people will go elsewhere.

CALEB. But . . .

JEREMIAH. It will be taken care of. I tell you things because you need to know them. You need to see how things work. It'll all make sense to you. You'll see.

CALEB. (*almost defeated*) I need to know what happened here. People's lives depend upon it.

JEREMIAH. People's lives depend upon many things. Damascus, Kansas is not one of them.

CALEB. Chapters need to be closed.

JEREMIAH. Chapters are closed. Caleb, chapters are closed. They're closed because they've already been written. Something written cannot be rewritten. It's done. People just don't like the way they ended. That can't be helped. They're done.

CALEB. Don't you think people need closure?

JEREMIAH. There's that east-coast psychobabble. Closure is a natural thing. It happens when it happens. You know that. It does no good to redo things already done. There is a future ahead, a big future. It'll take all our energy to make it happen, energy we don't want to waste chasing ghosts. Now, you have my word: all the residents here will have an extremely generous sum of money given to them for leaving. Then they can go spend it on the vices on their highway to hell.

CALEB.   And then?

JEREMIAH.   And then the burden of Damascus is no more.

CALEB.   You can just blot out the past?

JEREMIAH.   Caleb, there is no past. You can't go there. You can't touch it or look at it.
            You're not even 100% sure that its artifacts are actually remnants from the
            past or figments of some "group think."

CALEB.   You're telling me about "group think"?

JEREMIAH.   There is no larger "group think" than culture itself! Any and everything is
            groupthink. Think, man. Think!

CALEB.   You're going to wipe away a town and everything in it.

JEREMIAH.   You're not going to rest until I answer you bluntly. Yes. Yes, I am.
            Everything. Nothing left. Gone. It's a source of pain and regret and
            disappointment, and it will go.

CALEB.   I can't allow it.

JEREMIAH.   You can, and you will. There's too much at stake. There are things you
            don't want to visit here, stories you don't want to know, truths a bit too
            rough. And then there are people you have in your life who have done
            things that you don't want others to know about. You really don't want
            what they've done to destroy them. Leave it alone, Caleb. You're
            stubborn, and you're as sharp as they come, but just leave it alone. I'm
            protecting you, and I'm protecting the people you love.

CALEB.   Damascus.

JEREMIAH.   Founded by settlers who came from Kentucky in 1879. It boomed in those
            years. Damascus, Kansas. Named after the oldest city on the planet.

CALEB.   In Syria.

JEREMIAH.   Good ol' Damascus, Syria. It's been a while.

CALEB.   You've been to Syria?

JEREMIAH.   There's so much you don't know, son.

CALEB.   Enlighten me.

JEREMIAH.   In due time.

CALEB.   Why'd you go to Syria?

JEREMIAH.   Debts to settle. Issues to solve. More of the past.

CALEB.   And did you?

JEREMIAH.   Did I what?

CALEB.   Settle the issues there?

JEREMIAH.   No. I guess you could say they were left in limbo.

CALEB.   Jeremiah Coffee with another Damascus filled with unsolved problems?

JEREMIAH.   Another door to be closed.

CALEB.   Are you going after Damascus, Syria, too?

JEREMIAH.   No. I'm going to allow it to take care of itself.

CALEB.   I'm totally amazed. I can't believe I'm hearing any of this.

JEREMIAH.   I'm going back to Denver. You know where I stand. You need to get yourself in order and get your thinking straight. I'll be waiting on you. There's a lot you need to learn and a lot you need to know.

CALEB.   (*Cold.*) Good-bye, then.

JEREMIAH.   See you soon.

JEREMIAH exits. Caleb walks around for a few paces. Then he makes a barbaric scream.

DMITRI enters with an older woman by his side.

DMITRI.   Caleb?

CALEB.   What?

DMITRI.   Are you okay?

CALEB.   No. To be painfully honest, I'm not okay in any way.

DMITRI.   What happened?

CALEB.   I'll have to tell you when I calm down.

DMITRI.   I hate to do this, but I need you meet someone who needs to talk with you.

CALEB.   Did Elvis show up?

DMITRI.   (*excited*) Where?

CALEB.   It was a joke, Sta . . . I mean Dmitri. Who do I need to meet?

ROSA.   Caleb?

CALEB.   Yes, ma'am. Do I know you?

ROSA.   No, you don't, but I know you.

CALEB.   That seems to be the case around here.

ROSA.   Oh, Caleb. I'm kept up with you through the years. With all the people and all the groups of people who want the best for you.

CALEB.   I'm sorry, but I'm confused. Who are you?

ROSA.   Just a friend of a friend of the family. My name is Rosa Barrett. I've lived in this town all of my seventy-six years. And when you've been here this long, you know things.

CALEB.   That things?

ROSA.   Things that people keep quiet.

CALEB.   That seems to be everything.

ROSA.   Not everything, Caleb. I'm so glad you're here. I'm so glad someone is finally checking on things.

CALEB.   I want to. I want to badly. I just need help. Can you tell me: do you know what happened to my father, David Martinez?

ROSA.   I know who your father was, Caleb.

CALEB.   Do you know the events surrounding his death?

ROSA.   I know the stories, and I know the story that was told. I wish I could tell you what happened on that rooftop. I don't know if Jeremiah was there or not. I have my theories, but those are hard to prove, but I do know there was more to what Jeremiah wanted people to know.

CALEB.   What more?

ROSA.   Your grandfather was upset by the fact that David had joined the military, but there was something more than that. He was frantic, Jeremiah that is. He was angry and nervous several days before your father's passing. I remember it well. I had my suspicions because I knew some things that a very few of in town were privy to.

CALEB.   Go on.

ROSA.   Are you sure? When you open up the past, you may not like what it has in store.

CALEB.   At this point, I want to know the truth, no matter what it is.

ROSA.   Several years back, decades ago, your grandfather was a handsome young man. He was full of charisma and fire. He'd found himself under the wings of the Reverend RC Montgomery. The reverend had lost his only son, Abel in a military training accident, and he took to Jeremiah like a duck to water. He took him everywhere, even on a trip to the Holy Land. It was the talk of the town, how they'd done mission work, and actually travelled to the other side of the world. When they returned, Jeremiah was a little different, a little more distant, a little sassier than he had been. We just figured it was because he was a big world traveler now. We may have been right. Years went by. And Isabel married your father. Jeremiah did take to him. Please never think Jeremiah had it out of him. He didn't. He treated him like a son. And then something happened that he kept very hush-hush, something that he doesn't even know that some of us know about. But we do. Almost thirty years ago, a young lady showed up in town. She was beautiful. Olive skin. Long black hair. She was from Damascus. Not here. The old Damascus, the one in Syria. Her name was Maya. She was here a while. She was very quiet. She was here literally months. We all were very curious as to why this young lady would just show up in our small town, all alone. Then she started asking to see Jeremiah Coffee, telling people that he was her father, that he and her mother had met years ago on his trip to the Middle East, and that she was the result. As you can probably guess, Jeremiah was going to have none of that. He did meet with her. We knew that for a fact. And we know that something she had said eventually convinced him of her identity because she told Hazel, the lady she rented a room from said he broke and offered her some cash to help her. It wasn't long before her uncle from Syria showed up and whisked her back to their homeland. I can tell you from my own eyewitness account that Jeremiah went into a six-month depression. It was obvious to everyone that he was on his last leg emotionally. He flew to Syria for some reason, but came home even more down. Within a month, his wife, Mary Alice had a heart attack. It was bad. That's when the whole family decided to pick up and move to Denver.

CALEB.   Wow.

ROSA.   But, that's not all, Caleb. There's something more I hesitate to tell you, but if I were you, I'd want to know.

CALEB.   Okay.

ROSA.   Please don't get angry at the messenger.

CALEB.   I won't. I promise.

ROSA.   Before her uncle came and took her back to Damascus, she told Hazel and me something that Hazel took to her grave and I have never told a soul.

CALEB.   Yes.

ROSA.   She said that during the time that she was here, trying to talk with Jeremiah, trying to get things right . . .

CALEB.   Yes?

ROSA.   She and your father, David, had . . . seen each other. She was pregnant with David's child. Hazel received one letter a year later. Maya had given birth to a son, and Maya was pretty much shamed by her family. Caleb, Jeremiah doesn't know this, but you have a brother, and he's living in Syria.

CALEB is in shock.

While Rosa and Dmitri are frozen in their scene, Dr. Claudia comes DR and addresses Caleb as if he is in the audience.

BARKER.   Yes, I agree. You have to go to Damascus. This has to be solved. I'm so, sorry, Caleb. But I have faith in you. You have to make this right.

NATHAN.   (*Enters, crosses DL, addresses the audience in the same manner*) No. No, Caleb. It's insane. These are tough times. Travel is extremely restricted. It's a dangerous idea, and you don't know what's true and what's not.

BRADFORD. (*Enters, crosses L of Barker*) Nathan, tell your friend that he should be careful. There's no guarantee of safe passage. If he insists, let me know. We need to say a prayer for him.

DONNA. (*Enters, crosses R of Nathan*) I wish you would tell me what you found. I wish you would tell me where you're planning to go. I can't lose, you, too!

CALEB. (*Crossing DC*). Dr. Barker, I know. This has gone too far. There has to be answers somewhere, even if it takes me across the globe. Nathan, don't worry. I've been in tight fixes before. I don't know what I'm going to do. And please tell your pastor that I appreciate his prayers. I know. I know. He's your parents' friend. Grandma, I can't tell you too much. I can tell you that there a lot more than we ever realized. (*to himself*) I don't know what to do.

DMITRI. (*walks up and put his hand on Caleb's shoulder*) You have someone to find. I think you should go to Syria. It's sandy this time of year.

CALEB. I think you're right.

SCENE 48—CORRESPONDENCES

Isabel is standing, looking away from the audience. Jeremiah arrives.

JEREMIAH. Isabel. Why am I here?

ISABEL. Did you address that question in your university philosophy classes, Dad?

JEREMIAH. Are we really going to resort to sarcasm? You're far too old for that.

ISABEL. Yes, I am.

JEREMIAH. Why did you ask for me to meet you up here? I haven't been on the roof of the storage facility since we had it built fifteen years ago.

ISABEL. You know, the Rockies are absolutely beautiful. We see them every day and take them for granted. Have you ever stopped and looked at them afresh? Not worried how you've seen them in the past, but to take them in and see them as they truly are?

133

JEREMIAH.   Isabel, if you're going to talk in riddles, I'm going back down to my office. I have work to do. (*He turns to leave.*)

ISABEL.   I'm not stupid.

JEREMIAH.   Pardon?

ISABEL.   I said I'm not stupid.

JEREMIAH.   Did I ever say you were?

ISABEL.   Not in so many words.

JEREMIAH.   What are you talking about?

ISABEL.   You know, I followed in your footsteps. I went to Yale. I became a lawyer. I believe in what you believe in. I believe in it passionately and whole-heartedly, even the parts that make people hate us. I believe in you. I have always believed in you.

JEREMIAH.   What is wrong with you?

ISABEL.   With me? No. Not with me. I know, Dad. I know.

JEREMIAH.   Know what?

ISABEL.   What happened all those years ago. It's taken me a while. I didn't have all the pieces, but now I know.

JEREMIAH.   Years ago?

ISABEL.   Yes. With David. And with Donna.

Silence.

JEREMIAH.   You don't know what you are talking about.

ISABEL.   I found the letter. You know. The letter.

JEREMIAH.   Letter?

ISABEL.   The letter that David received from someone the day before he, the day before he was . . . (*pauses*) you see, I never knew why. I know you mentioned the suicide note and that you kept it from me to keep it from hurting me, but yesterday, yesterday, yesterday, I found something extraordinary. It was hidden beneath a board in the back of my closet: a

134

letter in an envelope. And do you know what that letter was? Do you? It was a threat, a letter of extortion, addressed to David, my David. And there was mention of some horrible things, and there were other things in the envelope. And I was sick, physically sick until I had a revelation, a revelation as clear as a stream of water. That note, that letter, it seemed so familiar, so very familiar. Dad, I've worked with you for my whole life. I know how you think and how your mind works and how you write. I know your patterns and structures. I know what happened. I'm your daughter. I know what you did, and I know how you did it. It's past, and it's over, but I know. I know.

JEREMIAH.   Is that all?

ISABEL.   Is that all? What are you asking? Am I going to *do* something? No. What can I do? Why would I? I just know.

JEREMIAH.   I'm going downstairs.

ISABEL.   Wait. I told you I know you. And I know your patterns and even your words. I know your words well.

JEREMIAH.   Yes?

ISABEL pulls out a collection of letters, the letters Jeremiah wrote Abel years ago.

JEREMIAH.   Where did you . . . ? How long have you . . . ?

ISABEL.   A very, very long time. A very long time. And yes, I've known, and I've read them. And I know. I know.

JEREMIAH.   Isabel . . .

ISABEL.   And I've kept them and protected them.

JEREMIAH.   What?

ISABEL.   But that time is up.

JEREMIAH.   What do you mean?

ISABEL.   Dad, I have known through the years, even when Mom was still alive. I've had them and kept them, but after this, after all this I've figured out, it's time to stop all this.

JEREMIAH.   What do you mean?

135

ISABEL.   I'm tired of harboring them. I'm tired of the burden. I am just tired.

JEREMIAH. And?

ISABEL.   You go on down.

She pulls out a lighter and catches the letters on fire.

JEREMIAH. Isabel?

ISABEL.   It's okay, Dad. You go down. When this is finished, I'll be on down, too.
           We have an empire to run.

Jeremiah stares and then numbly exits. Isabel watches the letters burn.

SCENE 49: IN THE LAND OF THE BLIND

Nathan and Dmitri enter, eating.

NATHAN.   Okay. I get it. You'll eat anything.

DMITRI.   It's just food. In my country, we ate a lot more than you do here. You're
           all too scared.

NATHAN.   I'm pretty daring, but I'll just take chocolate and maybe strawberry. It's
           ice cream, Dmitri.

DMITRI.   Yes, a palate for a variety of experiments.

NATHAN.   Just don't get it near me.

DMITRI.   It's just sushi.

NATHAN.   In ice cream. In ice cream!

DMITRI.   It's all good.

NATHAN.   Far from it.

DMITRI.   I'll teach you.

NATHAN.   That's okay. I'm good. Hey. Do you know if Caleb's heard from Betty recently?

DMITRI.   I know she called him a few days ago. It didn't go well. He wasn't happy.

NATHAN.   Well, damn. That sucks. Do you know when he's going to meet us?

DMITRI.   (*eating*) Oh, he's not coming today.

NATHAN.   He's not? Another audition?

DMITRI.   No.

NATHAN.   Rehearsal?

DMITRI.   No.

NATHAN.   Where is he?

DMITRI.   Syria.

NATHAN.   Oh, okay. (*Beat.*) What?!

DMITRI.   What?

NATHAN.   Did you say "Syria"?

DMITRI.   Yeah. He left yesterday afternoon.

NATHAN.   And you didn't tell me?

DMITRI.   You didn't ask.

NATHAN.   Damn, damn, damn. (*Starts to exit, walking rapidly, pulls out cell phone*) Ramsey, I need to talk with Stearman ASAP. No, it IS an emergency. (*Exits.*)

Dmitri slowly follows, eating his ice cream.

The stage darkens. CALEB, wearing dark black and brown clothes, including a large coat, walks stealthily across stage, looking in and out of homes and buildings. Two men quietly come up behind him. They shine a flashlight upon him.

SYRIAN MAN 1. ‏ما اسمك؟ (*pronounced "mā ismuka?"*) [*"What is your name?]*

137

Caleb does not say anything.

SYRIAN MAN 1. ‏ما اسمك؟‏ *(pronounced "mā ismuka?")* *["What is your name?]*

SYRIAN MAN 2. ‏ماذا تفعل؟‏ *(pronounced "mehza TES phalum")* *[What are you doing?]*

Caleb freezes.

SYRIAN MAN 1. *(with anger)* ‏ما اسمك؟‏ *(pronounced "mā ismuka?")* *["What is your name?]*

The men approach Caleb and begin to punch him. He tries to defend himself. As the struggle continues, one of the men pulls out a mace-like eye spray and sprays Caleb in the eyes. He screams and holds his eyes. One of the men takes the butt of his gun and hits Caleb in the head, knocking him out. They drag him offstage.

SCENE 50: SUNSHINE AND DAISIES

ELI.   Good evening, I'm Eli Connor, and you're watching Eye on the World, where we look where we're not supposed to look so you can know the truth around you. There's a lot going on on the planet tonight, so we need to get started. Today's opening statement: A planet on the brink. Tonight, terrorists hold greater territory and reek more horror than any other time in history. Rebel jihadists have taken over the city of Damascus, Syria. The President of Syria has fled to Turkey, and rebels have taken over the palace and the house of government. And even more frightening, they have control over the Syrian army and the stockpile of chemical and biological weapons. For years, our greatest fear has been for weapons of widespread death to make their way into the hands of irresponsible terrorists hell-bent on war. Tonight, our fear is a reality. The new leadership in Syria has warned Israel to sound its alarms because they will be hit soon. If and when that happens, I wouldn't want to be in Damascus. The US State Department has ordered all Americans to leave Syria at once. These are not good days. And the truth is not sunshine and daisies.

SCENE 51: THE MISSION

NATHAN PENNINGTON and HAROLD NEWFORD stand uncomfortably, waiting. Lt. Colonel MARK TAMBEROL enters the room. The marines salute. TAMBEROL returns the salute.

NATHAN.   Sir, what did you find out?

TAMBEROL. Well, it's bad. It's very bad.

NATHAN.   Is he alive?

TAMBEROL. Yes, but he's been beaten pretty badly. There were six armed men, and they basically ambushed him right outside the city limits on the southern edge of Damascus. With all the events going on on the international front, this was not the time for us to have a problem like this.

HAROLD.   Sir, do we know where he is?

TAMBEROL. Yes, we're pretty sure. He's in a small brick house in the one of the neighborhoods in the eastern part of the city.

NATHAN.   That's the old stranglehold of the jihadis.

TAMBEROL. Which makes it all the more dangerous. We are not even supposed to be in Syria at all now—officially. And now we have a man there.

NATHAN.   And we have to get him out.

TAMBEROL. And he shouldn't have been there in the first place. Washington is pissed on so many levels, trying to figure out all the details and why.

NATHAN.   We have to get him out, sir.

TAMBEROL. That's what I told the brass, Pennington. We can't let a civilian get taken like that, even if we claim there's nothing we can do. The fact that it's in the first twelve hours is a big help.

HAROLD.   And we are willing to jump on a copter right here on this freighter and go do what needs to be done, sir.

TAMBEROL. Hold your horses, Newford. Do you know why Martinez was even in Damascus in the first place?

NATHAN. There's no telling, sir. You know those Broadway stars. Their heads are in the clouds.

TAMBEROL. Well, his status in New York is sure a push in getting a rescue mission together.

NATHAN. So. there *is* a rescue mission in the works?

TAMBEROL. It's already planned. And you two are going in. (*Pennington and Newford smile at each other.*) That's what you get for befriending an actor.

NATHAN. And a lawyer.

TAMBEROL. (*shaking his head*) Is it too late to call it off?

SCENE 52: NO GREATER LOVE

The sound of a helicopter. If possible, the effects of the winds from the helicopter should be seen. In runs PENNINGTON, NEWFORD, and JONES, in rescue gear, guns in hand. They look around, go from house to house, securing the neighborhood, making sure no one sees them.

A woman carrying a baby walks by and freezes. Pennington puts finger to his lips to quiet her. She scrambles away silently and quickly.
Lights come up DL and we see the same events from scene one.

In slow-motion: PENNINGTON and NEWFORD in US military attire enter UC and, carefully looking around them, rush to the unconscious CALEB, check his vitals, untie him, de-hood him, and carefully begin to take him out the way they entered.

A kidnapper appears DL, shoots NEWFORD in the leg and kills PENNINGTON. NEWFORD shoots and kills the kidnapper. JONES runs in, gun up. The two soldiers exit, JONES carrying the CALEB, NEWFORD carrying the body of the fallen PENNINGTON.

SCENE 53: A WRETCH LIKE YOU

Several Elite Street church members sit around in chairs.

CHURCH MEMBER 1.   What a day!

CHURCH MEMBER 2.   I don't know when we've made so many new signs and folded so many brochures.

CHURCH MEMBER 1.   We're ready for Spokane, Los Angeles, New Orleans, and Madison.

CHURCH MEMBER 2.   And we have those smaller signs for the kids to use at that preschool.

CHURCH MEMBER 3.   I'm so glad we're done. It's pretty amazing.

CHURCH MEMBER 2.   Amazing is right.

CHURCH MEMBER 1.   (*singing*) "Amazing Grace!"

CHURCH MEMBER 2.   Oh, I haven't heard that in so long!

CHURCH MEMBER 1.   (*singing*) "How sweet the sound!"

Church Members 2 and 3 join in in harmony.

CHURCH MEMBERS 1, 2, and 3:   (*singing*) "That saved a wretch like me.
I once was lost but now I'm found.
'Twas blind but now I see."

They all laugh and clap. Jeremiah Coffee walks in.

CHURCH MEMBER 1.   Hello, Jeremiah.

JEREMIAH.   Don't ever sing that song here again.

CHURCH MEMBER 3.   What?

JEREMIAH.   I said don't ever sing that song here again.

CHURCH MEMBER 3.   Amazing Grace?

JEREMIAH.   It's a lie. And it's a trick of the devil. There's no grace for sinners. The wrath of God Almighty awaits them. That song teaches redemption for the masses and gives hope to the wicked. There's no hope. There are the elite. There are those of us He knows. That song is not to be sung in our midst.

CHURCH MEMBER 2.   Okay.

JEREMIAH.   Understood?

CHURCH MEMBERS 1 and 3.   Understood.

JEREMIAH exits.

SCENE 54: TWO ROADS DIVERGED

CALEB sits in a chair, his back to the audience. The room is silent. Dmitri enters. He approaches Caleb, carrying a cup of tea.
DMITRI. Here's your tea. (*Caleb doesn't respond.*) Caleb. Do you still want your tea?

Caleb takes the tea with his right hand.

DMITRI.   How are you feeling?

Caleb doesn't respond. Dmitri walks away from Caleb. It's obvious that he is worried.

CALEB.   I'm okay.

DMITRI.   Is there anything that I can get you?

CALEB.   No.

DMITRI.   Okay. (*Pauses.*) Oh, there were three TV reporters at the door again a few minutes ago. I told them you weren't ready to talk with anyone yet.

CALEB.   Thank you.

DMITRI.   And one of those celeb websites called my number. I guess they figured out our connection. They were asking questions about your grandfather. I pretended that I couldn't understand English.

CALEB.   Thank you.

DMITRI.   And Nathan's mother called.

CALEB.   Dmitri.

DMITRI.   Yes?

CALEB.   Not now.

DMITRI.   Okay.

CALEB.   (*standing, turning around. He wears a sling on his left arm and a patch on his right eye.*) I can't deal with it right now.

DMITRI.   Okay.

CALEB.   What was that depressing Russian song you were playing earlier?

DMITRI.   In all fairness, I didn't know you could hear that. I was trying to get some character work done.

CALEB.   Does your character commit suicide?

DMITRI.   I'm sorry.

CALEB.   No, I actually liked it. A lot. It clears my thoughts.

DMITRI.   (*Pauses.*) Is there anything you need? Anything I can do for you?

CALEB.   Can you kill someone?

DMITRI.   It's been a long time.

CALEB.   I'm not joking, Dmitri.

DMITRI.   You're under a lot of stress. You've been through a lot. More than anyone I've even known, and that's a lot!

CALEB.   I'm not going to ask you to do anything for me.

DMITRI.   I can! You need something to eat?

CALEB.   No, I mean I'm not going to ask you to deal with these other problems for me. I have to do this myself.

DMITRI.   You need to lie down again.

CALEB.   No, I'm tired of lying down. I'm tired of taking everything lying down.
            I've spent my life dealing with things I've had no control over. I've had
            enough. (*Pauses.*) Then something changes you. Something big changes
            you. I was in that little room. The binding was so tight that I couldn't feel
            my feet.

DMITRI.   You don't have to . . .

CALEB.   No, it's okay. It's okay. I was there, no water, no water. They didn't give
            me any water. And they didn't let me . . . I mean . . . I pissed myself. And
            I . . . And I couldn't sleep. Every hour, they came in and beat me. And
            someone came in with broken English and kept telling me that they were
            going to do something that I couldn't understand, until I made out the
            word "crucify." I don't know if I've ever been more scared. I don't know
            much more. It just hurt, hurt so bad.

DMITRI.   You're home now. You're going to be okay.

CALEB.   But at what cost? At what cost, Dmitri?

DMITRI.   Things happen. We don't know how things are going to . . .

CALEB.   But I should have. I should have. And others should have. There's no
            reason why they shouldn't know that what they do has major, major
            effects. And yet, they don't know. Or they don't care.

DMITRI.   I know.

CALEB.   Dmitri, I need to use your cell phone.

DMITRI.   Sure.

CALEB.   I need to find a flight to Denver tonight.

DMITRI.   Denver? Are you sure that's a good idea.

CALEB.   I'm going.

DMITRI.   Do you need me to go with you?

CALEB.   No. I'm going alone.

DMITRI.   I don't think the doctors will let you, and I know the defense department
            won't allow you to go anywhere now.

CALEB.   I'm going. It's not like I'm leaving the country. It's not like I'm some perpetrator. They see me as the victim. They're not worried about me right now. They have other things on their plate.

DMITRI.   Caleb.

CALEB.   Dmitri, I'm going to Denver. Tonight. And I probably won't be coming back.

DMITRI.   Caleb?

CALEB.   Your phone please.

SCENE 55: HIGH NOON

A hooded figure moves across stage. She pauses at the edge of a building and removes her hood, revealing her identity: Betty. She takes two deep breaths, takes out a gun, looks at it, and puts it back in her pocket.

Jeremiah enters from the other part of the stage. He is talking on his cell phone and does not notice Betty.

JEREMIAH. No, Richard. I'm not going to talk with them under these circumstances. (*Pauses.*) I know. Yes, I know. Publicity is priceless, but it depends upon the kind of publicity. (*Pauses.*) I'll talk with anyone anywhere as long I can control the message. (*Pauses.*)

Betty steps out nervously and takes out the gun. Jeremiah's stance is such that he cannot see her. She listens to his conversation then slowly brings the gun up and points it at Jeremiah's back. She is at least twenty feet from him.

JEREMIAH. (*continuing on the phone*) That's right. And you're to tell them no. They don't need that information. This country is a hellhole of vomitus excrement, but my family is sacred. (*Pauses*) They can do what they will, but I'm going to protect Caleb.

Betty, hearing this part of the conversation, slowly lowers the gun.

JEREMIAH. I love that boy, and I want the best for him. He's my grandson.

Betty stares at him in disbelief.
Jeremiah, having never noticed Betty, exits the stage the same way he entered, still talking on the phone.

JEREMIAH.   (*leaving*) I should be there in ten minutes. (*He is gone.*)

Betty remains, facing the place of Jeremiah's exit, holding the gun at her side. Unnoticed by Betty, Isabel enters and hits Betty over the head with a brick. Betty falls, unconscious. A man enters the same direction from which Isabel entered.

ISABEL.   Get her out of here. And have Nick get the van. I need two of you to get ready. You're taking her to New York—after we have a little talk.

SCENE 56: HOT TEARS

Caleb sits at his grandfather's desk. Silence. Jeremiah enters. He does not expect Caleb to be sitting there.

JEREMIAH.   Caleb.

CALEB.   Grandfather.

JEREMIAH.   Well, I must say that you actually caught me off-guard.

CALEB.   Imagine that. An upper hand I guess.

JEREMIAH.   I figured that you'd be dealing with quite a few issues right now.

CALEB.   You have no idea.

JEREMIAH.   It's not everybody that experiences such a trial by fire. It's a miracle that you're sitting here, boy.

CALEB.   I guess I'm just a marvel from God.

JEREMIAH.   (*with suspicion*) I guess you are. (*Three beats.*) How's your eye?

CALEB.   Temporarily blinded. Whatever I was sprayed with burned the cornea, but the doctors said it should heal in a matter of months.

JEREMIAH. Doctors. Modern men of science. "And such were the great men of renown."

CALEB. Indeed.

JEREMIAH. So, like I said, I didn't expect you here, at least now. Why'd you come to Denver? There are reporters everywhere storming the church, and I'm sure someone saw you come in.

CALEB. No one saw me.

JEREMIAH. Well, good. Why are you here? Have you had a chance to think about things?

CALEB. I sure have.

JEREMIAH. And do you see the possibilities? Do you feel the weight of your position?

CALEB. I do.

JEREMIAH. Why did you go to Damascus?

CALEB. We talked about this there.

JEREMIAH. No, not Kansas. Why did you go to Syria? Who did you talk to? Who filled your head full of stories? And I know good and well what those stories were. I'm not sure who told you what, but they're nothing but damned liars, out to spread the seed of Satan against the church of God.

CALEB. No stories.

JEREMIAH. I know better. Why did you go to Syria? (*Pauses.*) Why did you go to Syria?!

CALEB. You know that Damascus holds truth that needs to be told. It evidently always has.

JEREMIAH. The only truths that Damascus holds are half-truths and accusations. I've been there, boy. I've sought the truth there, and it's not to be found. It's a web of deceit and lies. And you put yourself at grave risk pursuing an apparition. You risked a very lucrative future. Your life is more important.

CALEB. Than someone else's?

JEREMIAH. Absolutely.

CALEB.   If you makes you feel better, I didn't find her.

JEREMIAH.   (*Pauses*) There is no "her." Caleb, there is no "her."

CALEB.   Okay.

JEREMIAH.   I'm serious.

CALEB.   Okay.

JEREMIAH.   And you came here to . . . ?

CALEB.   See you. There's so much that you really don't know.

JEREMIAH.   What do you mean?

CALEB.   Just making a statement. So much you're oblivious to. With all your power and anti-celebrity, and you still don't know.

JEREMIAH.   Son, I don't know what's going on in that head of yours, but I'm certain that you're still dealing with some effects the stress you've recently endured.

CALEB.   So much.

JEREMIAH.   Nonetheless, I neither have the time nor the patience to begin another round of your antagonism. If you truly want to discuss the future and what you are heading up to accomplish here, but if you're here to start another argument with me, I'm afraid that's not happening.

CALEB.   I know. (*He pulls out a gun.*)

JEREMIAH.   And what do you think you're doing?

CALEB.   What does it look like?

JEREMIAH.   It looks like you're being quite foolish.

CALEB.   It's over. I'm tired. There's so much deception and ignorance disguised as wisdom that it makes me sick.

JEREMIAH.   It makes me sick, too.

CALEB.   Stop twisting this.

JEREMIAH.   Why do you think we do what we do? This world is a sinful slush pit of immorality and stupidity.

CALEB.   I'm not talking about the world. I'm talking about here.

JEREMIAH.   Yes, you're talking about the world. You're projecting your frustration with life, with the lifestyle you've chosen to live, with all the people who've fed you lies, all of it on your family and this church.

CALEB.   That's not true. The pain and anger I have is not from the outside. It's from here. It's from you.

JEREMIAH.   I've never lied to you. I've always been honest with you. Even when you haven't liked what I had to say, even when you've hated what we do, I've never sugarcoated it. I have told you the truth.

CALEB.   No. You haven't. This is all one big lie. One big crazy experiment in cruelty and sadism. This whole world would be better off with you gone. I'll be better off with you gone.

JEREMIAH.   That's not true, Caleb.

CALEB.   Quit contradicting me. I'm about to end this once and for all.

JEREMIAH.   No, you're not.

CALEB.   Yes, I am.

JEREMIAH.   (*walking closer*) You're angry. You're angry because of all the things that you've seen and heard, and you haven't even been able to convince yourself 100% that any of them are true. And you're smart enough to know that assumption without proof is dangerous, Counselor. You know. You know this world is a horrible place with lies and selfishness and broken promises. And you know deep down inside that the promises I've made you are not going to be broken. You know. You know. We're blood. We're flesh and blood. And you know that the things I say and do, while not pleasant are right. You know. I'm your grandfather. And you know that.

Jeremiah slowly takes the gun from the numb Caleb.

JEREMIAH.   Now, you've been through a lot. Your mind is mush now.

CALEB.   (*through hot tears*) I hate you.

JEREMIAH.   Okay. But that'll change.

149

CALEB.   How can you be who you are?

JEREMIAH.   Years of practice. (*He starts to exit.*) Come with me. I'll have Richard find you a place to rest.

Caleb stands up slowly, stares at Jeremiah, and then follows him out.

SCENE 57: A TANGLED WEB

NEWSCASTER: (DR)   The Denver City Council will hold a public meeting concerning the issue one week from tonight at 5:30 p.m. at the City Council Chambers in the City and County Building. The meeting is open to the general public.

And on a final note, a small town says its last good byes. The town of Damascus, Kansas has sadly been on the decline for several years, but with the remainder of its last residents moving from the tiny hamlet, Damascus has become a ghost town. As a result, with the purchase of the town proper by developers, bulldozers came in today and began the process of taking down all the structures in town. There's no news yet as to what plans lie in store for the area, but people in neighboring towns say they welcome Damascans looking for a new place to call home. Years ago, the town had notoriety for being the home to the infamous Elect Street Church led by Jeremiah Coffee. But almost thirty years ago, Coffee picked up and moved his congregation and church operations here to Denver, where he has steadily garnered attention that many in the city have not liked. No one ever said freedom of speech is always pretty. (*exits*)

DMITRI.   (*DC, talking on his cell via speakerphone, holding it, leaving a voicemail*) Caleb, this is Dmitri. I don't know what's going on right now, but I know things are crazy. I hate to tell you this over the phone, but I want you to know that I'm going to go away for a little while. I'm going back to Russia. This city has been weird recently, especially with all that's been going on. I need to go home for a while. I haven't seen my dad in five years. It's time. We go through phases, right? I guess we do. I'll keep in touch. Take care of yourself. Please. Uh, good-bye. (*Exits.*)

BARKER: (DL) You are soon to be advocates. You will stand and bear the knowledge of the law of the land so that your clients will be fairly and fiercely represented. That means that you have to get the knowledge. No matter what you see on television and movies, you can't bluff your way through your practice of law. People's lives, people's families, people's livelihoods stand in the balance you are helping hold. If you take this profession lightly, if you think this is merely about stuffing your purse, if you think it's a grand joke, stop and change direction now. That's not what is about. It's about justice and making sure that people are treated fairly and that, every so often, mercy is offered. I make you this promise: after you finish your time here at Yale, you go off and practice law, and if I find out that you have violated the trust of the innocent and misused your power, I'll make it my personal mission in life to see you disbarred. This used to be a noble profession. It still can be. Now, if you're ready to begin, we have some knowledge to obtain in this class. I'm Dr. Claudia Barker, and I'm here to help you become a world-class lawyer. (*exits*)

BRADFORD. (DR) Yes, officer. My name is Jacob Bradford. I serve as pastor of the Saints Way Christian Fellowship here in Richmond. One of the members of my church is James Pennington, the father of the fallen marine, Nathan Pennington. James's wife, Lisa called me earlier this afternoon in a panic. It seems that James has been missing since last night. She has called his cell phone repeatedly and has elicited the help of her daughter and son-in-law to see if they can find him, but they cannot. As you can imagine with the throes of recent grief, she is beside herself. So, she asked me to contact you to report his disappearance. (*exits*)

ROSA.   (DR)--(*on the phone*) Donna? Donna Martinez? Oh, Donna, it's so good hear your voice. It's been such a long time. (*Beat.*) This is Rosa Barrett. From Damascus. (*Beat.*) Yes. No, it's okay. Don't worry. (*Beat.*) It's a long story. I had to do a lot of major detective work before I found a way to reach you. (*Beat.*) Seriously, don't worry. No, I don't have time to get into it all right now. Donna, listen. I have to get in touch with your grandson ASAP. Yes, Caleb. It's all right. No, I . . . You don't? I have to tell him something of the gravest importance. He came to Damascus before they dozed it under. (*Beat.*) Yes. He and I talked, and I told him something that was true, but I've found out something that he needs to know. (*Beat.*) I feel just awful. (*Beat.*) Yes. (*Beat.*) Oh, you do? (*Beat.*) Oh. I didn't know. I didn't realize. (*Beat.*) No, it's a letter that was sent to Hazel. (*Beat.*) Yes, Hazel. Remember? She rented a room out to . . . yes. (*Beat.*) Donna, there's a letter that we found before they took everything down. It came to her after she passed away. (*Beat.*) It was from Maya's sister in Syria. (*Beat.*) I didn't either. (*Beat.*) Donna, listen. Maya and her son are dead. They died years ago in an auto accident. (*Beat.*) I didn't know. (*Beat.*) I promise. (*Beat.*) I know. I know. (*Beat.*) Do you have any idea where I can find Caleb? I have to fix this. (*exits*)

As Rosa exits, we see James Pennington, wearing dark clothes, including an overcoat. He is standing, nervously in Jeremiah Coffee's office, examining various objects in the room. Jeremiah enters.

JEREMIAH. Mr. Pennington.

JAMES. Jeremiah Coffee.

JEREMIAH. Yes, that would be correct. Well, how interesting to see you here.

JAMES. Those are pretty much my sentiments as well.

JEREMIAH. With recent events, we turn away almost every who comes to the compound, but when I heard that it was you, that you'd come all the way from Virginia, I wanted to make sure you were escorted straight to my office.

JAMES. Yeah. I hope you'll forgive me that I don't know exactly how to respond to that.

JEREMIAH. The great Richmond lawyer at a loss for words?

JAMES. No. For sentiment.

JEREMIAH. Ah. (*Pauses*) I hope you don't mind my cutting to the chase, but it's pretty late and I'm pretty direct—in case you hadn't heard.

JAMES. I've heard.

JEREMIAH. Good. My grandson's alive. Your son died to make sure that remained so. I know. I have many mixed feelings about the situation, so if you came here to make sure I realize that, your trip was in vain. I'm aware of what happened.

JAMES. You're aware?

JEREMIAH. Yes. (*calloused*) I know the facts, down to each detail. I know what happened and that Caleb is alive because of it all. There's no need for us to hash out anything or to ask for some emotional response.

JAMES. You're serious?

JEREMIAH. About what? Of course, I'm serious. I don't know what you're referring to.

JAMES. Caleb is alive because of my son's sacrifice, BUT . . . ?

JEREMIAH. But nothing has changed. The world is as it is.

JAMES. You're a madman.

JEREMIAH. Perhaps to some. Someone quite different to others.

JAMES. I came here to kill you.

Jeremiah does not respond.

JAMES. Did you hear what I said?

JEREMIAH. I heard you.

JAMES. My son died a horrible death. He was taken from his mother and me at the most beautiful time in his life. He was full of life and energy and integrity and compassion, very much unlike you and your ilk, and you sent your thugs to his funeral, the very young man who saved your grandson, to say those vile, wretched remarks. I came here with every intent of killing you. Every intent. But I won't. It's not who I am. I just wanted to find out why. And I wanted to let you know how much I will speak out against your treachery for as long as God gives me breath.

JEREMIAH. Mr. Pennington, you are a man of letters. Harvard Law, right?

James nods in disbelief that he would seem to try to change the subject.

JEREMIAH. The law is a remarkable thing. It's both liberating and destructive. It allows for the grotesque anti-God actions of the world that you shamelessly and disgustingly defend.

JAMES. I . . .

JEREMIAH. No need to spout off your litany of cases. I know your career. I have read every single record of every single case you've been involved with. Every one. It's a wild and wicked world. You're supposedly a man of faith, and yet, you live in this world of putrid iniquity, making your money hand over fist. You are a member of the lost world. You're the hollow men, headpiece filled with straw. Empty, shallow, at a loss to defend your own son.

JAMES. What?

JEREMIAH. You heard me. You and your powerbrokers live in a fallen world that embraces every perversion known to man, being permissive and tolerant of death and murder and pain, and too fearful or too stupid to stand up for things that are right.

JAMES. You don't know anything.

JEREMIAH. I know a lot, James. A lot more than you realize. I know why you came here. You need that chapter closed. You need me to listen to you and to convert to your sinful way of viewing the world. You want me to apologize to you and make nice, tell you that I'm sorry that I held up the little signs that hurt your sensibilities.

JAMES is in utter shock, every word of Jeremiah ripping at his already weakened, grieving soul.

JEREMIAH. You want me to "change my ways" and embrace the way of mercy and kindness and global redemption and love everybody and sing "Kum Ba Ya" while we hold hands and drink sodas in a daisy chain of sweaty perpetuity.

JAMES. What? (*further weakened*)

JEREMIAH. You want me to tell you that it's going to be all right. Well, it won't. You want to tell you that I've sorry. Well, I'm not. You want me to tell you that my image of God is wrong. Well, it's not. You want to tell you that I am appreciative of the glorious gift your son gave for my grandson and that I should never have sent my people to stand at his funeral. Well, I won't. Your son is dead. He is dead, James. He is not coming back.

JAMES sinks into Jeremiah's desk chair. He is devastated. With each of Jeremiah's words, he breaks down further and further, putting his head in his hands, his face covered.

JEREMIAH. Caleb is coming around. We're nursing him back to health, and he is starting to come around to the right way of thinking. He's going to a warrior for right. He was saved to come here and keep this church alive, to keep truth alive. Your son is gone forever. He was part of this wicked society, this evil system that fights against God. He was a soldier for the "pervert" regime, and he paid that price. He died for a sinful, pathetic nation, and he is gone forever. You won't see him again. Your wife won't see him again. Even his new little nephew will never have known him. He was doomed, just like you. Your only son is dead. Enjoy your life, paying the price for your sin. Without your son.

JAMES cries. Jeremiah looks at him and shakes his head.

JEREMIAH.   It's late. I have places to be. My assistants have already gone home.
When you get finished with your little cry, please turn off my light and
shut the door. I have to step next door for a few minutes. When I return, I
need for you to have left. And don't leave any tears on my desk. Save
those for Richmond.

*Jeremiah exits. James sits, head down, crying. After a few seconds, he hits the desk with
both fists. Head still down.*

JAMES.   Damn you!

*He continues to cry but rubs his face with the arm of his coat, trying to wipe tears. A
figure in a dark enters and stands across from James.*

JAMES.   Leave me alone. Haven't you said enough?

FIGURE.   I've had quite enough of you.

JAMES.   (confused, wiping his face with his sleeves) What?

FIGURE (DONNA).   When you get to hell, remember that Donna Martinez sent you
there, Jeremiah. Burn forever.

JAMES. (starting to look up) Wait.

Donna shoots him three times. He collapses face down, face concealed. She exits calmly.

James dies at Jeremiah's desk.

SCENE 58: THE PRODUCT

REPORTER. (*In a frenzy*)   Good morning. I'm reporting to you live from Jerusalem.
We have earth-shattering news. If you've been watching
news or have connected to your media at all, you know that
yesterday afternoon, northern Israel was hit with dozens of
missiles authenticated to have been carrying chemical and
biological agents. Multiplied thousands are dead. Early
yesterday afternoon, the current leadership in Damascus
claimed official credit for that attack, promising more

deaths in the Jewish state. Well, it seems that Israel has not taken the attack or the threat lightly. We're reporting. Oh my . . . We're reporting that some sort of major, and we mean major attack was launched against the city of Damascus itself overnight, a major attack with seemingly one detonation. The oldest city on the planet. And it seems that Damascus has been hit hard, hard enough that we are having trouble finding it possible to find sources in the area to talk with. Whatever the retaliation for the chemical and biological attacks, if the retaliation was indeed from Israel, it was devastating and Biblical in proportion. As we find out more, we'll keep updated. Keep us in your thoughts.

Broadcast news music blares. Eli Connor, in a suit, is sitting at his desk. As the music subsides, Connor begins.

ELI.   Good evening, I'm Eli Connor, and you're watching Eye on the World, where we look where we're not supposed to look so you can know the truth around you. There's a lot going on around the planet tonight, so we need to get started. Today's opening statement: Where to begin? As you've heard, the world is in chaos tonight. We know that multiplied thousands were killed in northern Israel yesterday, and we assume the attack on Syria is retaliation for the missiles. We aren't certain about the fate of Damascus. We know something that has happened, and we've been programmed to assume the worse. Our guest tonight is someone who knows a little about Damascus. As you remember from a few months ago, Caleb Martinez, professional actor, Yale-educated lawyer, and grandson of controversial hate-mongering minister Jeremiah Coffee was held hostage before being rescued by marines, one of whom lost his life.   Martinez has recently been recovering from his injuries and is reportedly being groomed to take over the infamous reigns of leadership from his grandfather in coming years. We want to hear from him about Damascus and what it means to him and to find out why he's following in Coffee's footsteps. But first, my thoughts. Freedom of speech is a remarkable gift given us to speak our minds and share our feelings. In this country, we are guaranteed the right to share our ideas even if others find them repulsive. That's where our guest plays in. His family, his church pushes the limits of our tolerance, but isn't that what free speech does? We'll explore this and more with Caleb Martinez. Mr. Martinez, thank you for being here.

CALEB.   Thank you, Eli.

CONNOR.   At any time, we have to shift our focus to Damascus, so let's get to the point. Why are you embracing the ideology of your grandfather? And what are your plans?

CALEB.   Eli, if I may? How many people are watching this show?

CONNOR.   On any given night, four million. Tonight, with breaking new, maybe double. But we're not here to grandstand for . . .

CALEB.   Hear me out. I promise not to grandstand.

CONNOR.   Speak your mind, Caleb.

CALEB.   My name is Caleb Martinez. I am a son and a grandson. I'm a lawyer and an actor and a friend. I've said and done many wrong things. I'm a combination of everything I've seen and done. The past year of my life has been unlike anything I'd have ever imagined. I've been places I never want to see again. I've seen people I never care to see again. I've lost people. I've lost positions. I've seen this world that my grandfather has taught me is evil and full of corruption and full people he says are hopeless and unable to share in the mercy of God. I've been taught about it all, how there is no chance for good or for this thing called love. And I've been groomed to take over and fall in the footsteps of Jeremiah Coffee. But I'm here to tell you, all of you, millions of you, that I Caleb Martinez denounce the evil that is Elect Street Church. I denounce the teachings of Jeremiah Coffee. His kingdom is a domination of power and money, manipulation, shaming, and threats. His means is hatred and his weapon, biting words.

During the course of the Caleb's next words, the following events from Scene 1 play out again:

From SR, we see a shadowy figure which looks remarkably like JEREMIAH COFFEE. He walks in an arc toward C, when an ambiguous figure appears, following him. The first man stops, looks at the SR pulpit. The second figure pulls out a pistol and shoots him. He falls. Immediately, a police officer appears SR and runs up to the fallen man as the ambiguous figure, this time walks down stage, reveals his identity to be Dmitri, then runs UC and then exits UR.

CALEB.   My name is Caleb Martinez, and I am my own man. You can hate me for my family. I don't choose my blood. You may hate me for my careers, but I am who I am. I'm unashamed of my choices. I am a graduate of Yale. I am an actor. I have friends I love and know people I can't trust. And though my grandfather has perverted the love of God, I still believe in God and His mercies. If any of this bothers you, so be it. But I won't change it for you, to fit your definition of who you want me to be so that your world can make sense. I won't be controlled or defined. Yes, this world can be horrible at times. There is a lot to be ashamed of and upset by, but the solution is not more hatred. *(Church members, dressed in all white, walk out holding up signs that are completely blank, totally white.)* The solution is not signs of hatred and cruelty. I'm Caleb Martinez, and I will not follow what I'm told has to be. I'll follow what I know to be

157

right, and be who I know I am. (*The church members turn their backs to the audience and face upstage. Their signs are still raised.*) I'm Caleb Martinez, and I'm not a victim of blood. I'm a product of grace.

A still image of an explosion is seen during Caleb's last, few words. Then all goes to black.

Lowery Christopher Collins (Chris) has been an educator and writer for over thirty years. He is currently a professor of English at Panola College in Carthage, Texas. He has taught at the high school, middle school, and elementary school levels and as an English and literature instructor at the college and university level. For several years, he was a high school theatre director and a gifted education consultant. He's been honored with several teaching awards, including the Young Audiences of Northeast Texas Outstanding Service to the Profession Award and the Kennedy Center's Steven Sondheim Award for being one of the most "Inspirational Teachers" in the U.S.

He is also an award-winning playwright of over thirty scripts, a weekly newspaper columnist, a short story writer, a poet, a pianist, a vocalist, a songwriter, a recording artist with Daywind Studios, the founder and artistic director of Stagelands Theatre Company, an aspiring novelist, and a (former) choir director. He's taught a variety of classes, from rhetoric and composition to literature to acting to the Bible.

He holds a Bachelor of Arts Degree in English and History and a Master of Arts Degree in English from Stephen F. Austin State University in Texas and has served on fine arts and gifted education committees as well as on a board of governors for a small playhouse.

In addition to his interests in teaching, directing, and writing, he has a fondness for lighthouses, windmills, filmmaking, salsa, sculpture, Flannery O'Connor, travel, dominos, guacamole, social media, genetics, Maine, landscaping, pillows, gospel music, Shakespeare, marbles, YouTube, quantum physics, movies, weird jokes, maps, trees, cold rooms, and Texas.

He can be reached at mrchriscollins@hotmail.com,

on Facebook at www.facebook.com/tofferdreams,

on Twitter at "tofferdreams,"

and at his website: www.ChristopherCollinsOnline.com.

To view Christopher Collins's books and other writing, visit Ponderlake Publishing, at www.ponderlake.com.

Made in the USA
Columbia, SC
18 May 2020